D0335570

Hunky Dory

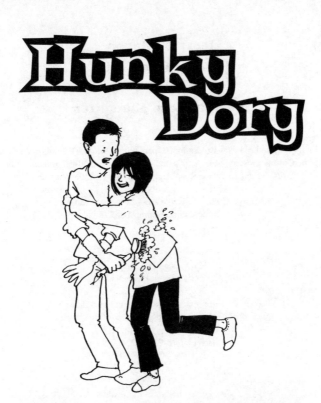

JEAN URE

Illustrated by Karen Donnelly

HarperCollins *Children's Books*

Jemma Mason
Rachel Cornforth
and
Amelia Rose Slaughter

First published in Great Britain by HarperCollins *Children's Books* in 2007
HarperCollins *Children's Books* is a division of HarperCollins*Publishers* Ltd,
77-85 Fulham Palace Road, Hammersmith, London W6 8JB

The HarperCollins *Children's Books* website address is
www.harpercollinschildrensbooks.co.uk

1

Text © Jean Ure 2007
Illustrations © Karen Donnelly 2007

The author and illustrator assert the moral right to be
identified as the author and illustrator of this work.

ISBN-13: 978-0-00-722460-9
ISBN-10: 0-00-722460-5

Printed and bound in England by
Clays Ltd, St Ives plc

one

I am having terrible trouble with girls. They won't leave me alone! This morning in geography this girl in my class, Amy Wilkerson, deliberately came and sat next to me. I mean, like, out of about three zillion empty seats she had to come and park herself next to *me*. Why did she do this? It was extremely embarrassing, especially when she started getting all cosy and leaning up against me so she could talk to her friend Sharleen on the other side of the gangway. Why didn't she go and sit next to Sharleen? That's what she normally does. Why does she want to come squashing herself all over me?

I really like geography, it's one of my favourite classes, but how can you concentrate when there's someone nudging you all the time, and breathing over you, and banging at you with their knees? She ruined it for me! I couldn't get away from her. Plus she's left-handed, so whenever we had to write stuff our hands kept touching. I'm sure they didn't have to keep touching. If she hadn't been hunched right up close to me they wouldn't have. It was almost like she wanted them to. So now I've got a messy page in my geography book where my handwriting suddenly jerks up and down where she's jogged me. I try to keep my stuff tidy. I don't like it all messy! I hope she doesn't think she's going to make a habit of this, cos if she does I shall have to—

I don't know! I don't know what I shall do. It's getting beyond a joke! Amy Wilkerson is not the only one. The other day, in art, Janine Edwards kept beaming at me. I'm not imagining it! Every time I looked up, she caught my eye and she beamed. What was she beaming for???

It's quite scary. They're all at it! Beaming, breathing, *giggling*. It's even happening with Year 6. On my way out of school this afternoon there was a great gaggle of them, hanging around by the main gate. I recognised some of them from when I was in Juniors; I think they may be friends of the Microdot (otherwise known as my sister). When they saw me they all started to giggle and squeak and stuff their hands into their mouths. It's very off-putting when girls behave like that. I had to keep looking at myself in shop windows to check I'd got my clothes on right. I still don't know what they were giggling at. It makes me very self-conscious.

Maybe that's why they do it? Maybe it's their secret weapon. They get together in groups and lurk about, waiting for boys to giggle at. But why pick on me???

I didn't mean to write all that. All that about girls. They are not part of my plan and I don't know how they got there. From now on I am going to ignore them. They are going to be **KEPT OUT**.

Right. That's it! They've gone. Now I can get started on what I was going to get started on before I was interrupted. By *girls*.

What follows is the official autobiography of my life so far. So far as I have lived it, which is eleven years plus nine months, three days, and probably a little bit extra, only I am not sure of the exact time I was born as Mum says she can't remember. She just says vaguely that it was "in the early hours of the morning".

That is typical of Mum! She is quite a slapdash sort of person. Anyway, however long I have lived it makes a total of *at least* one hundred and eight thousand and forty-four hours (not counting leap years). That might not seem a lot to some people – my granddad, for instance, who is almost eighty – but I think I have lived long enough to make a start. One day when I am famous as an expert on dinosaurs, people might be quite curious to read about my early struggles. Not just with Amy Wilkerson but with my family, and especially with the Microdot. Getting them to take me *seriously*. That is my biggest struggle.

Now that I have started, I am not sure what to put in and what to leave out. There is not much to be said about my beginnings; they were just quite ordinary. There isn't anything much to say about where I live, either. That is also quite ordinary. A bit depressing, really, though I do my best not to dwell on it. I'm sure that lots of people who are now famous had what Dad calls "humble oranges" (he means humble origins; it is Dad's idea of a joke. He is always coming out with these things).

I suppose I should say something about where I go to school, except that I can't really think of anything much worth saying. School is also just ordinary! But one day people might be interested. I think I shall make *headings*.

School
Easthaven High.

I am in Year 7, and these are my favourite lessons:

Geography
Science
Maths

These are my *least* favourite lessons:

French
PE
Cross country running. (This is not really a lesson but we have to do it once a week and it is like a form of torture.)

I expect I would quite enjoy English if we could read more interesting books, instead of the rather soppy ones that Mrs Baxter always goes for, and I would definitely like history if we could do the Triassic Period, but Mr Islip says this is not on the curriculum as no one knows enough about it. Pardon me, but I know enough about it! I bet I could do an entire exam on the Triassic Period. Just because Mr Islip is ignorant, I don't think he should accuse other people of being so. He didn't even know when the Triassic Period was! He thought it was only about two million years ago. When I told him it was *twenty-three* million, he just said, "Well, there you are. That proves my point." Actually, all it proves is that even teachers don't necessarily have any idea what they're talking about.

Anyway, that is enough about school. On the whole it's not a bad sort of place. The worst thing about it is where it is: right next door to the Juniors. This means that the Microdot and her friends can gather and giggle every day if they want, and there is nothing that I can do to stop them. And there is no other way of getting out of school! Not that the Microdot was actually there when they were giggling, but I wouldn't be at all surprised if she was the one that organised it.

"Go and wait by the gates until my brother comes out and then start giggling!"

I can just hear her. It's just the sort of thing she'd do. I'm not going to ask her about it; I wouldn't give her the satisfaction. And if she dares ask *me*, like, "Did you notice my friends when you left school today?" I shall simply say, "Friends? What friends? I didn't know you had any." I mean, what were they giggling *about*?

Now I have gone and upset myself again. I think I shall make a list. Any list! List of my family.

My Family

Oliver Jones. My dad.

My dad is very long and thin, with big hands and feet which people tease him about. Recently he has developed a bald patch on the top of his head. He is very sensitive about his bald patch, so that sometimes he combs his hair over it in a vain attempt to stop it showing. Mum says he is being ridiculous. "A man of your age!" Personally I think that is a bit unfair, cos how would she like to go bald?

Dad is a wood sculptor. He works in his shed in the back garden, sculpting wood into strange and curious shapes. People pay him for this. When they are not paying him – when there are not enough people who want bits of wood in strange and curious shapes – he makes rustic furniture for the local garden centre. Once for my birthday, when I was little, he made me a wooden dinosaur. He was really supposed to be making a rocking horse, but he said, "The wood wouldn't let me". Often, according to Dad, you just have to make what the wood tells you to make. So I got a rocking dinosaur, instead, and that was what set me off on the whole dinosaur trail. I have Dad to thank for it!

Sara Jones. My mum.

Mum is almost the exact opposite of Dad, being very short and a bit on the plump side, with a round beaming face. Everyone says that she is pretty, and I guess she is, though it is hard to be sure when it's your own mum. Certainly, in spite of being plump, she is a really fast mover. She whizzes about all over the place like she is jet-propelled. Dad is for ever telling her to "Just stay still for a minute, woman! You're making me feel giddy".

Mum, I think, is a bit eccentric; she is definitely not like other people's mums. Not the ones that I have met. For instance, she hates cooking, she hates housework, she hates shopping, and most of the time she wears old jeans and sweaters covered in hairs. Animal hairs. Actually, the whole house is covered in animal hairs. Sometimes they even get into the food. It is all very disgusting, but what can you do? I don't think Mum even notices.

When she was first married, Mum used to be a veterinary nurse. Now she runs a cattery in the back garden (opposite Dad's shed) where people leave their cats when they go on holiday. There is a big wire enclosure with a row of little huts, each with its own snuggle bag and litter tray. Even its own scratching post and catnip toy. Dad says it is like a five-star hotel.

One of the maddest things about Mum is her passion for Jack Russells.

She started off with one and now she has five. Every time she hears of a Jack Russell that needs a home, she goes racing off to get it. There are Jack Russells all over the place! On the chairs, on the table, on the beds. Last week one even jumped into the bath with me. It's kind of zany, but you get used to it.

William Jones. My brother.

William is fifteen, and is tall like Dad, but not so thin. I think he is probably quite good looking, or will be when he has grown out of his pimply phase. Will's pimples cause him much distress. He has special cream  to put on them but so far it doesn't seem to have done much good. His life, just at the moment, is dominated by pimples. I feel very sorry for him and just hope it never happens to me.

Dorian Jones. Myself.

I think I have said enough about me for the moment. Obviously there will be more later on.

Annabel Jones. My sister.

The Microdot takes after Mum, being so short she practically can't be measured. Like Mum she is always *busy*; but while Mum scuttles about like a demented hen, all mad and happy, the Microdot hurls herself to and fro in a frantic rage, like a porcupine with its quills stuck up.

I call her the Microdot to pay her back for calling me

Doreen, which is what she does when she wants to annoy me. The Microdot suits her. Annabel is a ridiculous name for someone that's hardly any taller than a milk carton. She says Dorian is a ridiculous name full stop.

"Specially for some geeky nerd that's into dinosaurs!"

I have a lot of trouble with my sister. I am not going to say any more about her; it will only get me all hot and bothered again. I *know* she was behind the giggling.

I am not going to think about it.

Grandparents

Mum's mum: Wee Scots Granny.

Wee Scots lives in Glasgow, and as we are down south – "true Sassenachs", as she calls us – we don't get to see her all that often. Which I think is a pity, as she is what is known as *a character*, meaning that she is even madder than Mum. She is also smaller than Mum, and rounder than Mum, but if they ever had a mum-and-granny race I'd back Wee Scots any time. She goes like the wind! She is the origin of my catch phrase,

Great galloping grandmothers! I use this phrase all the time. I am famous for it. I have this mental picture of all these ancient old grannies, galloping along. Wheeee! There goes another one.

Wee Scots would beat the lot. She is full of energy! Even though she is sixty years old she still bombs around on a moped. "Fattest woman on a moped in Glasgow!"

If Mum hadn't put a stop to it she'd probably bomb down here on a moped, as well. As it is, she comes by coach, arriving hot and flushed with too much usquebaugh (pronounced ooskabaw). That is the Gaelic word for whisky, and is what Wee Scots always says when Mum accuses her of having "tippled".

Dad's mum and dad: Gran and Granddad.

There is not a lot to say about Granddad as he is a rather quiet sort of person. He is also very old (he is the one that is almost eighty). He likes to play old-fashioned games that he played when he was a boy, such as *Ludo* and *Shove Ha'penny*, which he keeps in a cupboard. We always have to play them when we go to visit. I don't mind, if it makes him happy. I think when you have lived as long as he has, you deserve to be happy.

Gran – Big Nan – is not quite as old as Granddad, but I still can't think of much to say about her. She is very strict, and is always reminding us to watch our manners. She says that nobody under the age of fifty seems to have any these days. It bothers her quite a lot.

She and Granddad live in Weymouth, which is not very far away so we see them quite often, but fortunately only one day at a time. They don't come to stay. They came once, for Christmas, a few years ago,

but Gran couldn't take Jack Russells all over the place.
Dad says the Russells are our secret weapon!

It occurs to me that I might not have been quite fair

to Gran and Granddad, but it is very difficult, sometimes, when people are old; you can't tell what they are really like. You can't imagine them, for instance, ever being young. I have just tried to imagine Gran being in Year 6 and giggling. Or being in Year 7 and sitting herself next to a boy and *breathing* over him. No way! It is like trying to picture the Queen going to the toilet. The mind bogles. (Or is it boggles?)

I can imagine Wee Scots. I bet she scared all the boys rigid! I wonder if Mum did? I wonder if she used to giggle at Dad? Maybe I'll ask him and find out. I'd like to know if he had the same trouble I do. I didn't have it last term! Why has it suddenly started? *And how long is it going to go on?*

I'm getting worked up again. I shall finish my list! I've done Family, what else can I do? Dogs! I could do dogs. After all, they are part of the family.

Jack Russells

Molly, Polly, Dolly, Roly, and Jack. They are mostly white with brown splodges except for Roly, who has a black patch over one eye, and they are all mad and busy, just like Mum. They bark a lot and run around and jump on things. They also dig holes in the garden and play tug with people's knickers and underpants and bury chew sticks under cushions so that when you sit down you go "Ow! Ouch!" and wonder what is sticking into you. They are what Dad calls "dogs with *attitude*".

I have just thought of something else to add to my list and that is *friends*. I have two of them. Well, I have lots of people I am friendly with, but only two that are best mates. They are:

Rosemary Jones, who is my Uncle Clive's step daughter, which is why we have the same surname. I usually call her the Herb, as she hates the name Rosemary. In return, she calls me DJ, or Deeje.

She is kind of shortish and stubbyish, with blonde hair which she wears in spikes. Even though she is a girl, we get on really well. She does sometimes giggle, but not in an embarrassing kind of way, and she never does that screechy thing that lots of girls do, like when one of the Russells jumps up and scrapes her leg or puts great dollops of mud all over her. Most girls would go *shrieeeek! Ow! Look what it's done!* but not the Herb. She doesn't mind getting muddy. She doesn't mind her legs being scraped. She doesn't mind getting rained on or falling off her bike and banging her head. For a girl, she is all right.

She lives just round the corner, and as we go to the same school and are even in the same year (though not in the same class) we see each other pretty much all the time.

My other best mate is **Aaron.** Aaron Chandler. I have known him for ever. He is a small, knobbly kind of person. Knobbly knees, knobbly wrists. His face is covered in freckles and he has bright orange hair the colour of carrots. Carrots is what I used to call him, back in Juniors, until he said to me one day that he didn't think I should, as it "wasn't politically correct", so after that I didn't do it any more. I couldn't really see what was wrong with it, like I couldn't see that calling someone Carrots was insulting or anything, I mean what's wrong with carrots? But he is my friend and I didn't want to upset him.

Me and Aaron not only go to the same school but are in the same class. We hang out with Calum Bickerstaff and Joe Icard, but Joe and Calum live way over the other side of town so out of school we don't meet up that often. It's usually just Aaron and me – and the

Herb. The Herb's like an honorary boy; she joins us most of the time. Aaron reckons she's OK.

Actually, I'm a bit worried about Aaron. He wasn't in school today, which was how Amy Wilkerson got to park herself next to me. If Aaron had been there, she wouldn't have dared. I just hope he's back tomorrow! I can't cope with this; it's all too much. I don't want another messed up page in my geography book!

Why can't all girls be like the Herb?

two

Thursday

LIKES AND DISLIKES

Name your favourite

Food *Maggot pie and chips*

Drink *Wet sick*

Colour *Puke green*

Song *Mr Smelly Goes to Town*

TV programme *Secrets of a Sewage Farm*

Band *Flaming Flamingos*

The Microdot gave me this questionnaire. She said she

was doing tests, and I had to fill it in. So I filled it in, and she screamed at me.

"This is just *stupid*!"

Actually, I thought it was quite funny, but the Microdot has no sense of humour. She screeched, "I suppose you think you're being clever?"

I guess I might have smirked a bit. Not exactly meaning to; more like a sort of nervous tic. It does my head in when she screeches. Trouble is, once she starts she can't seem to stop. She just rages on and on. She screeched at me that it wasn't clever, it was *stupid*.

"There isn't any such programme as Secrets of a Sewage Farm, and if it was it would be disgusting!"

I said, "Pardon me, that is just your interpretation."

"What about maggot pie? Are you trying to tell me that's not disgusting? And what's this stupid Flamingo thing? I've never heard of a band called that. You just made it up!"

I said, "How do you know? You don't know the name of every band there's ever been."

Witheringly she said that nobody would call a band anything that stupid. "It's just about the stupidest name I ever heard!"

I told her that that was the fifth time she'd used the

word stupid. I said, "You ought to get a bit more vocabulary."

She screeched, "Yes, and you ought to get a life! You know what this shows, don't you?" She snatched up the questionnaire and waved it at me. "It shows that you're *repressed*."

I said, "Yeah?" I don't think she even knows what the word means.

She said, "Yeah! It shows you're too scared to reveal your true self... you have to hide behind being *stupid*."

"That makes the sixth time," I said.

"Sixth time *what*?"

"Sixth time you've used that word."

"That's cos it's the only one that describes you!"

All because I treated her silly little questionnaire as a joke. I bet even if I'd taken it seriously she'd still have said it showed there was something weird about me. She's always saying I'm weird. She told me the other day I was like a human hermit crab.

"Skulking in your shell!"

If I'm like a hermit crab, she's like a hornet, all angry and buzzing. *Zzz, zzz, zzz! You're stupid, you're weird!*

I'm not like a hermit crab; I don't skulk. She just can't bear it when other people don't share her interests.

Shopping, and shrieking, and *giggling*. I reckon she ought to learn to be a bit more tolerant.

Now she's threatening to give me more of her idiotic tests. She gets them out of girly mags. *Ten Ways to Tell if a Boy's Interested in You.* (Like any boy ever would be, the way she carries on.) *Check your Popularity. Check your Street Cred.* It's all rubbish! She'd better not try any of them on me. She tried one on Dad the other day. Something about hair. *What your Latest Hair Style reveals about You.* Dad practically hasn't got any hair. Will said, "What it reveals is that Dad is going bald." She didn't have a go at *him*. She didn't accuse him of being stupid. It's just me she's got it in for. Her and her tests!

If she gives me that one about *Check your Popularity* I shall refuse to answer it. I don't see why, just because she's my sister, she should be allowed to humiliate me.

Friday
Aaron came back to school today; he said he'd been off with earache. I told him what had happened with Amy

Wilkerson, parking herself next to me and breathing over me. He drew in his breath and said, "I'd keep an eye on her, if I were you. Gobbles boys up for breakfast, that one. Obviously fancies you. It's what they do, they come and breathe over you, and touch you... did she touch you?"

I said, "She kept nudging me with her knee."

"See, this is what I mean," said Aaron. "She fancies you! She's got her sights set on you... *donk*!" He shot out the first two fingers of both hands, straight into my face. "It's like smoke signals, you gotta be aware of the signs. You gotta know how to respond."

I said, "I don't want to respond!"

"No, but if you did."

"I don't!"

"Can't say I blame you," said Aaron. He sucked in his cheeks. "Amy Wilkerson! Have to be careful with that one."

I wish now that I hadn't mentioned it to him. Aaron is one of those people, he always claims to know everything about everything. But you can't actually rely on him. Like the time he told me that a prendergast was someone that molested children, and for ages I believed him and wouldn't go into the newspaper shop cos of the lady in there being called Mrs Prendergast, until in the end Mum wanted to know what the problem was, so I told her, and she laughed and laughed and explained that Prendergast was just a perfectly ordinary surname like Smith or Jones and nothing whatsoever to do with molesting children. Aaron had got hold of the wrong end of the stick. *As usual.* It was very embarrassing.

I refuse to let him embarrass me again! When it comes to girls, I'm not convinced he knows what he's talking about. I don't believe that Amy Wilkerson fancies me. Why should she? I've hardly ever spoken to her. I reckon she was just, like, doing it for a joke. I bet what it was, her friend Sharleen had dared her. I bet that's what it was! Like the Microdot getting all her friends to hang about at the gates and giggle. Just to upset me.

On the other hand, who told Janine Edwards to keep beaming? There can't be two of them that fancy me! I don't want to be fancied; I just want to be left alone!

I'm really glad it's Friday; I am beginning to feel *persecuted.*

Wee Scots is coming tomorrow. That should be liven things up.

Saturday

Wee Scots arrived this morning, bright red as usual with the usquebaugh. Mum went to fetch her from the bus station. As they came through the front door Dad said, "Watch out, here she is, Hell's Granny!" Wee Scots bashed him with her handbag and cried, "Och, awa' wi' ye!" They have a really good relationship.

After lunch, while me and the Microdot were

doing the washing up, which is one of the tedious tasks we have to perform in order to get any pocket money, the Microdot said she'd got a secret to tell me. She said, "You know my friend Linzi?"

I didn't, but I didn't bother to say so; I just grunted. The Microdot has so many friends I can't keep up with them. Last year for her birthday she invited twenty people. Boys, as well as girls. She claimed they were "all my friends". I can't understand why she's so popular; she is *very* bad-tempered.

"My friend Linzi?" She snatched a plate out of my hand before I'd even had time to put it on the draining board. She always treats washing up like it's some kind of competition. "The one with the plaits?"

When she said that, I had this faint uneasy feeling come over me. I'd noticed a girl with plaits in the middle of the gigglers. She'd been giggling along with the rest, but more in a sort of embarrassed way. Grudgingly I said, "What about her?"

33

"She's got a crush on you."

"What?" I was so alarmed I let a glass go slipping through my fingers on to the kitchen floor.

"Now look what you've done," said the Microdot. "You've gone and broken it." Like I needed her to tell me? "That was Granny's favourite usquebaugh glass."

I said, "It's not an usquebaugh glass. She uses tumblers for usquebaugh. This is a water glass."

"It's still broken."

"I can see that, thank you very much!"

"Yes, well, anyway. Like I was saying… about Linzi. She's got this massive crush on you."

I said, "What d'you mean, *crush*?"

"Crush! Like she wants to *crrrrrrush* you!"

Before I knew what was happening, the Microdot had flung both arms round me and was squeezing me to a pulp. I said, "Geddoff!"

"I'm just showing you what she'd like to do to you. She'd like to *hug* you! And *kiss* you. Aaaah… it's so sweet!"

"Why don't you just shut up?" I said.

"Cos I want you to know how she feels. She's in love with you! Only she's too shy to tell you, so I thought I would."

I said, "Is that what all the stupid giggling was about?"

"Yes. It's really pathetic! They've all got crushes on you... they think you're so cute!" She gave this great cackle, like she was inviting me to join in. "But poor Linzi, she's got it worse than anyone. She is totally *gone*. She is, like, *demented*. She's written your name all over, everywhere! I've told her what you're like, but she just can't stop herself. I feel *sooo* sorry for her."

Crawling round the floor with the dustpan and brush, keeping my face hidden because I just knew I'd gone bright beetroot, I said, "So what did you tell her I was like?"

"Well, like you are... peculiar! Anyone that spends their time digging holes in the back garden and playing about in the mud... where's the sense in having a crush on someone like that?"

This is what I mean about my family, and the difficulties I face. Scorn and derision at every turn. I don't *play in the mud* and I'm not just digging a hole, I am *excavating*. It is serious work. They know this perfectly well; I've told them over and over. It is an archaeological *dig*. But the Microdot still treats me like I'm some kind of geek. Even Mum and Dad have a secret giggle – well, not all that secret, either, cos I heard them the other day telling someone about "Dory's hole", like it was just totally hilarious. It is an uphill struggle, in this house, trying to make something of yourself. One day when I'm Sir Dorian, and famous for my work on dinosaurs, they'll look back and feel ashamed of the way they treated me.

Of course I might be famous as a Crime Scene Investigator. That's another career I'm thinking of pursuing. I reckon I'd be good at it, as I find it most interesting on television when they examine the contents of people's stomachs or collect maggots and bugs that have taken up residence inside dead bodies. The Microdot says I am gruesome. She says it is totally disgusting and would make any normal person feel sick, but that is just her point of view. Mine happens to be different.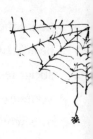

Anyway, if I'm peculiar so is she. She screamed her head off the other day, all because there was a spider walking across her bedroom ceiling. She screeched, "Get rid of it, get rid of it!"

I've told her about a hundred times that spiders are perfectly pleasant and harmless creatures, just going about their business.

"What d'you think they're going to do, bite you?"

She screeched that they might fall on top of her while she was in bed. They might even get into the bed.

"They could get down my nightdress!"

How peculiar is that? Fantasising about spiders getting down her nightdress. What makes her think any self-respecting spider would want to? I can't understand it when girls start freaking out at the sight of anything with multiple legs. The Herb came across a centipede the other day; *she* didn't freak. But then the Herb is different.

I spent the whole afternoon excavating. I've only got till the end of the month, then the builders are coming in to build Dad's new workshop, so I'm trying to get as much done as I can. Aaron and the Herb are helping me: they are my official assistants. I am doing my best to train them, but I have to say it is uphill work. They don't seem able to grasp the fact that there is more to excavating than simply picking up a trowel and digging as fast as you can. I've told them, you have to dig slowly. You have to dig carefully. You have to *sift*. Then if you find anything, you have to label it, and say where

it was, like how far down, and how far in. The Herb
asked me today exactly what it was we were hoping to
discover. Before I could give a more scholarly reply,
Aaron had jumped in and yelled, "Dinosaur bones!"

"What, in Warrington Crescent?" said the Herb.

Aaron said why not. They'd have stamped about in Warrington Crescent same as they did anywhere else.

"In the *back garden*?"

"You gotta remember," said Aaron, "it was all primeval swamp in them days. That's what it still is, deep down. Then the bones kind of work their way up. Prob'ly quite near the surface, some of 'em. I wouldn't be surprised if we came across the odd one now and again."

I said, "I would." This is exactly what I mean about Aaron always claiming to know everything when in fact he knows nothing. I said, "I'd be very surprised."

"So what are we *searching* for?" demanded the Herb.

I had to explain that it wasn't dinosaur bones, which in any case would be fossils by now, but just whatever turned up. So far I have discovered:

An old coin dating from 1936

A piece of broken china (a shard, as we professionals call it)

A small blue bottle (probably contained poison)

A rusty penknife, almost certainly antique.

Coin c. 1936

bottle (poison?)

Penknife

They are all cleaned up and properly labelled. I showed them to my assistants, thinking they would be impressed – thinking they might actually learn something – but the Herb just giggled and Aaron said, "Is that it?"

I said, "This is history, this is."

"Some history," said Aaron.

The Herb giggled again. Everything's always a big joke with her; she finds it very difficult to take things seriously. "You never know," she said, "it could be the scene of a hideous crime. We've got the murder weapon!"

"If you're talking about that penknife," I said, "it wouldn't go in deep enough." I know about these things; I've studied them.

"All right, then!" She snatched up the bottle. "Poison!"

It was all they needed. Next thing I know, they're both going mad with their trowels, showering earth in all directions. I told them quite sharply to stop.

"This is not the way you're supposed to do it! You're ruining the site!"

Aaron panted, "We're looking for a body!"

"You've got to admit, bodies would be interesting," said the Herb. "More interesting than bits of broken china."

I had to be very stern with them. I mean, yes, OK, body parts would be great. Teeth, or skulls, or thigh bones. I'd like to discover body parts just as much as anyone else, but it's *not the way that it's done*.

"If you're going to help, then help properly," I said. "Just try to be a little bit professional."

The Herb mumbled "Professional, professional," and stroked an imaginary beard, while Aaron went into exaggerated slow motion with his trowel. I said, "That's better. You're worse than the dogs!"

Dad has erected a special wire netting enclosure for the hole. He did it so that Mum, in her daffy way, wouldn't go trundling down the garden with a barrow full of used cat litter and fall into it, but it also serves to keep the Russells at bay. I do love the Russells, but I sometimes can't help wishing Mum had developed a passion for a more useful breed of dog. Dogs that could fetch, or carry, or herd. If the Russells got into the hole it would be total chaos. As it is, they all sit on the other side of the netting and whinge.

"Dunno why you don't let 'em in," said Aaron. "Get the job done far quicker."

44

"Wouldn't be professional," said the Herb. "Hey, I just thought of a joke! Is it OK to tell jokes?"

I think I must have hesitated, cos she said, "It's all right, it's a professional joke… it's a *dinosaur* joke."

"Yeah, yeah, go on!" said Aaron. "Tell it!"

"Right. What's a dinosaur that's had its bottom smacked?"

"I don't know," said Aaron. "What is a dinosaur that's had its bottom smacked?"

The Herb said, "A dino*sore*-arse!" She looked at me, triumphantly. "Funny?"

"Your mum wouldn't think so," I said. "She'd say you were being vulgar."

The Herb gave one of her cackles. "Rude, rude, Mum's a prude!"

"I reckon it's pretty good," said Aaron. "Here!" He gave me a nudge. "You tell the Herb about Amy Wilkerson?"

Herb said, "Ooh, another joke?"

"She fancies him," said Aaron.

"*Amy Wilkerson*?"

"Yeah, she went and sat next to him and started breathing over him."

"Yuck, yuck, *yuck*!" said the Herb. She turned, and made vomiting noises. "Amy Wilkerson... *puke*!"

"She's not that bad," said Aaron. "I've seen worse."

"OK then, you have her," I said.

"Yes, you have her," said the Herb. "Amy Wilkerson... *bluurgh*!"

I really wish I'd never mentioned it. I'm certainly not going to say anything about the Microdot and her gang of gigglers. It's funny, though, I never knew the Herb had it in for Amy Wilkerson.

When we went back in for tea I found Wee Scots doing things with mothballs. Threading string through them and tying knots.

"She's making necklaces," said Will. "To go round trees."

I said, "What do trees want necklaces for?"

Wee Scots cried, "Mothball necklaces, laddie!"

I screwed up my nose and looked at Will. Solemnly,
he said, "It's to stop the dogs using them as toilets."

And the Microdot says *I'm* weird?

three

Sunday

She said to draw a house and garden. I drew a house and garden. She looked at it and said, "That's supposed to be a *house*?" I said yes. I have never claimed to be any good at drawing.

She told me that I'd done it the wrong way round. She said, "Look at it! It's back to front."

Sometimes she is just totally illogical. How can a house be back to front? I explained that it was simply seen from the rear. She said, "So who draws a house seen from the rear? Honestly! It's so anti-social. It's like turning your back on people."

I said, "That is just your opinion."

"It isn't an opinion," she said. "It's *psychology*."

Huh! I bet she doesn't even know how to spell the word. She says she's going to give me one test a week until she's built up a profile. "Then we shall see!"

I told her she wouldn't see anything if I refused to do them, but she said that was where I was wrong. "If you refuse to do them it'll simply show you're scared."

I said, "Scared of what?"

She said, "Of having your true self revealed! So whether you do them or whether you don't, we shall still *see*."

I think this is a form of bullying. I told her so, and she said, "How can I bully you? I'm only ten years old."

"Which is far too young," I said, "to know the first thing about psychology."

"I'm *learning*," she said. "Ten isn't too young to start learning. Or to fall in love! Poor Linzi is *heartsick*. She's *suffering*. I'm really worried, cos she's my best friend – one of my best friends – and I'm just so frightened for her. If you keep on rejecting her like this—"

I resented that. I said, "I'm not rejecting her!"

"Excuse me," said the Microdot, "you walked

straight past her the other day. You didn't even look at her!"

"Cos I didn't even see her!"

"That's even worse! Not even *seeing* her. Like she's invisible! If I told her that," said the Microdot, "I dread to think what she might do. She might do something really awful. And if she did, *you'd be the one that was responsible for it!*"

This is definitely getting beyond a joke; it's putting me under a lot of stress. I don't know how much more of it I can take!

Monday

This morning at breakfast, in sickly sweet tones that practically oozed a trail of treacle right across the table, the Microdot announced that she was becoming "ever so worried about Dory". I knew at once that she was up to no good. I glared at her, but she just smirked and wrenched the marmalade away from me. Turning to Mum, still all sweet and sickly, she said, "You don't think he needs his eyes tested, do you?"

Mum, of course, latched on to it immediately. She is such a sucker! She said, "What makes you ask?"

"Well, it's the way he keeps missing things," said the Microdot.

"What things?"

"*People*," said the Microdot.

"Och, he jist has his head in the clouds," said Wee Scots. "He's a bit of a dreamer, aren't ye, laddie?"

"You'd think he'd notice *girls*," said the Microdot.

Wee Scots gave one of her throaty chuckles. (Mum says it's all the usquebaugh.) "I bet the girls notice him all right! I'd have noticed him when I was a wee lass."

"Dunno why you'd bother," said the Microdot.

If Dad had been there, he might have come to my rescue. Will was sitting opposite and I tried to catch his eye so that we could pull faces at each other, but he just went on cramming his mouth with cornflakes and refused to look at me. I think he should have done: after all, he is my brother. We ought to stick together!

Did some digging after tea. Aaron and the Herb came round and I gave them the house and garden test. The Herb said, "Ooh, do we get marked out of ten?" I said I would tell her after she'd done it.

Aaron got a bit stroppy and said he thought we weren't supposed to have time for anything except digging. "Way you were carrying on the other day, all bossy and *got to be professional*."

I had to soothe him. I said, "These are important psychological tests."

To be honest I think they are rubbish, but it is very undermining when a person of ten years old keeps telling you that you are weird and peculiar and anti-social. I really needed some kind of reassurance. I'm feeling a lot happier now; now that I've seen what Aaron and the Herb came up with. If I'm weird, they're even weirder. I mean, how's this for whacky: the Herb drew a house with a *face*. She said, "I wanted to make it seem friendly." Personally I thought it looked a bit

like Humpty Dumpty, but Aaron said it was more like something in a graveyard. He said, "That's morbid, that is."

He could talk! All he'd drawn was a mound, with antennae and aerials all over it. Not a door or a window to be seen. When I asked him what it was, he said it was an underground bunker for hiding in. The Herb said, "Underground bunker's not a house."

"Would be," said Aaron, "if you had to live in it."

"Why would you have to live in it?"

"Well, like if there was an attack, or something."

The Herb looked at me and slowly shook her head.

"Means I've got an instinct for self-preservation," said Aaron.

The Herb said, "Yeah? What about me?"

"You just want to be cosy and make nests."

he Herb froze. I saw this glint come into her eye.
 you saying I'm *girly*?"

"Nah!" Aaron backed off, double quick. The Herb can be quite dangerous when anyone accuses her of being girly. "Nah, that's not what I'm saying!"

"So what *are* you saying? Exactly?"

"I'm just saying you're, like… friendly."

"So what was all this about nests?"

Aaron's nostrils flared. I could almost see the beads of sweat break out on his brow. As team leader, I knew I had to step in.

"Let's just forget about it," I said, "and get back to work."

"Yes." The Herb gave Aaron one last simmering glare. "Let's be *professional*."

Aaron turned and began digging, frenziedly. I was about to yell at him to slow down when he suddenly cried out in excitement, "Great gobbets of mud!"

I thought for one wild moment he might have uncovered something interesting, but all it was was an old rusty tin.

I told him to do a label for it and put it with the other stuff. He said, "Can I write who found it?"

I said that he could as I believe it is important to encourage people. He was obviously very proud of digging up his tin, especially as the Herb hasn't dug up anything at all so far. He worked really well for the rest of the evening, without any of his usual grumbling. I was quite pleased with him.

All the trees now have little ropes of mothballs hung round them. It kills me!

Wednesday

This morning, as I'm packing my bag for school, I hear Wee Scots' voice calling urgently to Mum: "Sara, Sara, there's a dog on the table!" I meet Mum on the landing. I say, "There's a dog on the table." Mum says, "I heard." As we go down the stairs together, Wee Scots runs frantically along the hall.

"Sara, Sara, come quick! There's two dogs on the table!"

By the time we reach the kitchen, they're all on there, walking about amongst the cereal bowls. Polly's got a piece of toast in her mouth, Roly's wrestling with a cereal packet. One of them's knocked a milk carton on the floor, but it's OK, it hasn't burst. Jack's about to

close his mouth over the butter so I zip in, smartish, and wrench it from him. Mum yells at them to get off, and they all scatter.

Wee Scots goes, "Dogs on the table!" like she can't believe it. Mum remains unflustered, probably because she's used to dogs on the table. They haven't always done it, and I cannot now remember when they started.

When Jack came, probably. He wasn't with us last time Wee Scots paid us a visit. But it's definitely not normal, five Jack Russells on the breakfast table, no matter what Mum seems to think.

Suddenly, in that moment, I have a blinding revelation: it is the women in this family who are weird! Not the men. The *women*. What with Mum thinking it's

OK for dogs to be on the table, and Wee Scots hanging mothballs round the trees, and the Microdot—

I turn to look at the Microdot. She's dumped a shiny pink plastic case on the table and is lovingly poring over the contents. They are *all pink*. Nothing but pink! It's what she's spent her pocket money on. Little fiddly bits to put in her hair. Little dangly bits. Little glittery bits. Clips, combs. Bangles, bracelets. Everything *PINK*.

She catches me watching her and says, "What's your problem?"

I tell her that I haven't got a problem. "It's just come to me... I'm not the one that's weird, it's you. I mean, look at all that junk!"

She says angrily that it's not junk. "It's stuff I need!"

"It's *pink*."

"So what?"

I say that pink's girly. You wouldn't catch the Herb wearing pink! Not that I say that bit to her. The Microdot instantly goes into shrieking mode. She wants to know what's wrong with being girly.

"I am a girl, in case you hadn't noticed! Least, I thought I was. Maybe I'm not, and no one's told me. Maybe I'm a stupid *boy*. D'you think I'm a boy?"

I say no, I'm sure she's not a boy. "Boys wouldn't waste their money on that sort of crap!"

She shrieks, "It's not crap, you sexist pig!"

By now, all the dogs are barking excitedly and running to and fro across the kitchen floor. Wee Scots cries out that we're doing her head in. Mum bawls at us to shut up.

"Just stop it, the pair of you! Dory, leave your sister alone. Anna, stop screeching!"

The Microdot screeches that she's not screeching. She then picks up a pink thing and hurls it at me.

"Sexist *pig*!"

She is definitely not normal.

Thursday

Tried to do a bit of digging after school today with Aaron and the Herb, but Aaron was in a silly sort of mood and just wanted to mess about and tell stupid jokes like, "What do you call a man with a shovel?" To which the answer, apparently, is Doug. Which I didn't get and the Herb had to explain.

"D-U-G. *Dug*."

That's supposed to be funny???

"What do you call a man without a shovel? *Douglas*!"

"Dug-*less*," said the Herb. "Geddit?"

I said, "What's to get?"

"It's a play on words," said the Herb. "Listen, I've got one, I've got one! What do you call a girl with slates on her head?"

"I don't know," said Aaron. "What do you call a girl with slates on her head?"

"Ruth!"

"OK, what do you call a man under a pile of leaves?"

"I don't know, tell me!"

"*Russell*."

They went on like that the whole time. I'm not surprised at Aaron, cos he's got the brain of a flea, it hops about all over the place, but I was disappointed in the Herb. I thought she knew better. She is becoming very frivolous just lately.

And I have just worked out that one about the girl with slates on her head. *Roof*. I still don't think it's funny.

Friday

I have been ambushed! I was talking to Aaron, on our way out of school – actually I was telling him about the Argentinosaurus, which is the largest dinosaur known to man – when we heard this strange, high-pitched squeaking like a colony of bats. Aaron immediately stopped and said, "Wossatt?" I told him not worry about it. I already had bad feelings.

"Wot is it?"

It was coming from behind some big shrubby things which cluster by the gate.

"There's a load of girls," said Aaron.

I said yeah, it was where they hung out, and gave him a shove. I was about to explain to him how the Argentinosaurus was the height of a four-storey building and the length of two school buses, which are the sort of facts I should think anyone would be glad to know, when suddenly, from out of nowhere, jet-propelled, a body came hurtling towards us and threw itself on the ground in front of me.

I am glad to report that I didn't hesitate: I simply stepped right over it.

"Twelve metres," I said. "*Twelve metres*. You've got to admit, that's pretty damn tall! And twenty-three metres long. That'd stretch from here to about… I dunno! As far as the traffic lights, maybe?"

Aaron said, "Yeah… maybe."

"Maybe even further. Maybe right down's far as the High Street." I jerked at his arm. "What d'you reckon?"

He said, "Yeah. I dunno. Maybe. What d'you think she did that for?"

I said, "Who knows? Just felt like it, I s'ppose."

I managed to drag him away, but it was a nasty moment.

What cheek! What utter nerve! The Microdot has just had a go at me. She says I'm heartless and unfeeling.

"Poor Linzi faints at your feet and you just leave her *lying* there!"

I said, "She didn't faint, she chucked herself down on purpose."

"She fainted! She has a *crush* on you. This is the sort of thing that happens when people have crushes on people. You'd think you'd be *grateful*. I've never heard of anything so cruel… just walking on and leaving her! She could have had a heart attack. She could have *died*."

I said, "Yeah, and so could I. I could have tripped over and broken my neck. And don't tell me you didn't put her up to it cos I know perfectly well that you did!"

The Microdot tossed her head. "So what?"

"So it was totally irresponsible. *Stupid* thing to do!"

She flushed, angrily. "As a matter of fact it was a *test*, if you want to know. And you failed it! There's obviously something wrong with you. You obviously have a hate thing for girls."

I don't have a hate thing for girls. I know that they are necessary, and if they were all like the Herb we would get on fine. The Herb doesn't beam and gush and make a nuisance of herself. She doesn't persecute me!

I am feeling quite bothered. I think I shall have to make a list.

List of all my Dinosaur Books:

On the Trail of the Dinosaur

The Age of the Dinosaur

Talking about Dinosaurs

Back to the Dinosaurs

Facts about Dinosaurs

The Big Book of Dinosaurs

The Encyclopaedia of Dinosaurs.

I also have six books on fossils, four on prehistoric mammals and two on being a CSI.

I did all this from memory! I am feeling a bit calmer, now.

Saturday

Wonders will never cease! This morning, while we were cleaning out the cats' litter trays, which is our special Saturday task, the Microdot said she wanted to talk to me. I almost told her not to bother, as I thought she was going to start shrieking again, but for once she was quite restrained.

She said, "I want to ask you something... You don't *really* hate poor Linzi, do you? cos she loves you most terribly! *She* doesn't think you're geeky. She thinks you're really hot! Lots of people do, you'd be surprised. *I* was surprised, cos after all, I know you. They just go by how you look. It's wrong to judge people by their looks! I've told her this. I've told her, it's what's inside that counts, but she is just, like, totally *gone*." The Microdot clasped one hand to her chest and swayed dramatically with a scoop full of cat litter. *Used* cat litter. She said, "Know what she said?"

I said, "No. What?" I was busy keeping an eye on the cat litter. I didn't fancy great wet dollops of it landing all over me. "What did she say?"

The Microdot gurgled, happily. "She said you remind her of that man in *The Mummy* film... that one where they go down into the tombs and all horrible things come alive and jump out of their coffins and start chasing them? And then there's that bit where people's flesh all hangs off them and th—"

"Yeah, yeah," I said, "I saw it! What man are you talking about?" I was quite interested to know, as I thought it was a pretty good movie. Not that the ancient Egyptians are what you'd call *old*. But at least it showed people doing some serious excavating. "What's his name?"

She screwed up her nose, trying to remember. "Brenda?"

"*Brendan*. Brendan Fraser." Hah! He was the hero. "She thinks I'm like him?"

"Well, sort of. I mean, he was more into *action*. I can't exactly see you being into *action*. But she has this, like, daydream, where she's down in the tombs and you rescue her?"

I said, "Rescue her from what?"

"Those beetle things? Like in the film? Ones that burrow under your skin and go zizzing round your body and eat up your brain… she thinks it'd be really neat!"

"What, to have beetles eating her brain?"

"No, you idiot! You rescuing her."

I said, "Oh. Yeah. OK."

"I mean, you *would* rescue her," she said, "wouldn't you?"

I said, "Absolutely!" Fortunately I don't think any brain-eating beetles actually exist in this country, so I reckon I'm probably safe.

"You wouldn't just walk past and leave her? Like you did when she fainted?"

I was about to say – again – that she hadn't fainted, she'd hurled herself on the ground, when I caught a glint in the Microdot's eye and thought better of it.

"Brenda Fraser wouldn't walk past and leave her. She thinks you're better looking than Brenda Fraser. Which wouldn't actually be hard," said the Microdot, "considering he's, like, really ancient. On the other h—"

"Excuse me," I said. "Where exactly is this leading?"

"Not leading anywhere," said the Microdot. "Just thought you'd like to know. Most boys'd be flattered, being told they were better looking than some big hunk movie star."

"I am," I said. "I'm very flattered."

"Really?" The Microdot beamed up at me. Boy, was she in a good mood! "I'll tell Linzi. She'll be ever so pleased!"

"Yeah? Well, good! It's been nice talking," I said.

She said, "It has, hasn't it?"

I don't know what to make of it all. It's not often I get to have a civilised conversation with the Microdot. I'm still not sure what the point of it was, but it seems to have made her happy.

I wonder if Egyptian mummies are considered less geeky than dinosaurs?

four

Sunday

This is the latest test she gave me. She says it's the paint splotch test.

"It's simple! All you have to do is just look at it and say what you think it means."

I was tempted to say, "Means Mum's been at the paint again."

Dad says Mum shouldn't be allowed anywhere near a paint pot. She goes mad! She paints everything in sight, including the dogs. The dogs go pretty mad, too. They tread in the stuff, and sit in the stuff, and rub up against it while it's still wet. Then we have paw prints, and bottom prints, and furry skirting boards, and Mum's like, "Oh, God, get them out of here, get them out of here!" Any normal person would make sure they were shut away before they began, but not Mum. I really *don't* think the women in this house are normal.

Anyway, I didn't say what I was tempted to say cos I knew the Microdot would only start yelling. She was already working up to it. Jigging about and huffing.

"Well?"

I said, "Well... " I was being careful here; I didn't want her getting ratty. "Well, I..."

"All you've got to do is just *say*," said the Microdot. "You don't have to stop and think about it."

"What if I get it wrong?"

"You can't get it wrong. There isn't any *wrong*. Just look at the splotches and say what you think is happening."

"OK. It's someone being chased... someone trying to get away."

The Microdot went, "Hah!" And then she gave this derisive snort and said it again. "Hah!"

"What?" I said. "What?"

"I might have known!"

"Known *what*?"

"That that's what you'd say!"

By now, I might as well admit, I was becoming considerably annoyed. Even when she told me I couldn't get it wrong, she still wouldn't let me get it *right*.

"See, there's two different types," she said. "There's *friendly* types and there's *un*friendly types. The friendly types say it's someone running *towards* people, and the unfriendly types say it's someone running *away* from people. You're one of the unfriendly types. You can't help it, it's not your fault. It's just the way you're made," she said, kindly.

The fact she said it kindly made me even more annoyed.

"This is such a load of crap," I said.

"It's not crap, it's psychology! And you know you're not allowed to use that word… *crap*."

I said, "Crap, crap, double crap!" She gets me like that. "I suppose *you're* one of the friendly types?"

"Well, I am friendly," she said. "I like people."

"I like people!"

"You don't like Linzi."

I shouted, "I never said I didn't like her!"

"Yes, you did, and don't shout!"

I said, "I am NOT SHOUTING!"

"You are, you're deafening me."

"Well, you deafen me all the time, and I didn't say I didn't like her. When did I say I didn't like her? I'm the one that's supposed to be rescuing her from beetles!"

She tossed her head. One of her *most* irritating habits. "*Supposed* to be."

"I'd do it," I said, "if I had to. The opportunity, however, has not yet arisen." I thought that was rather good: *the opportunity has not yet arisen.*

Her lip curled. "Don't see how it can when you still haven't even asked her out."

Asked her out??? She actually thought I was going to *ask her out?*

"Go figure!" said the Microdot.

I have just got it. I have just twigged. I might have known she had some ulterior motive, giving me all that guff about being better-looking than Brendan Fraser. That girl is just *so devious.* Talk about low cunning! It's the last time I let *her* engage me in conversation.

I wish I knew how she curled her lip like that. Hers goes right up in a hoop; mine just kind of twitches. She must have very prehensile lips. Yeah, and a very prehensile brain! *What can I say that would get my geeky brother to date my best mate*? The answer to which is: nothing! Absolutely nothing! I'd have to be desperate before I went out with anyone the Microdot was friends with.

Tuesday

Something very horrific happened at school today: I got shut in the gym cupboard with Janine Edwards. I still can't work out how the door came to close on us. *Or* what Janine was doing there in the first place, considering she was supposed to be in the sports hall with the rest of the girls. And how come the light went out? I guess she must have panicked and knocked against the switch cos suddenly we were in darkness and she started screaming. Next minute she's hurling herself at me with such force I'm staggering backwards into a bunch of string bags containing netballs, and before I know it I'm down on the floor, struggling to get up, being smothered by string bags and this great lumping girl. Not meaning to be sexist or anything, but Janine Edwards is *big*. I honestly thought she'd gone mad and was trying to strangle me. You hear of these things.

It was Mr Hoskiss that wrenched the door open. He is not as a rule my favourite person, being this hideous sports fanatic that makes us all run mindlessly round muddy fields in pouring rain and force ten gales, but for once I was quite relieved to see his big beefy figure towering there. Another minute squashed beneath Janine Edwards and I might not have been alive to tell the tale. Unfortunately, as well as Mr Hoskiss, half of 7S were there. The *male* half. All standing gawping. They seemed to find it very amusing, me being trapped in a cupboard with a girl on top of me. Aaron and the others, later, made some quite uncalled-for remarks which I do not intend to record as I am doing my best to forget them.

Arrived home this afternoon to find that the Microdot had brought the Linzi person back with her. She is a little pink podgy thing like a beachball. Mum and Wee Scots can't stop cooing over her; they say she's "a real wee cutie". The Microdot looks at me, very hard, as she introduces us.

"Linzi, this is my brother, *Dory*. Dory, this is my friend *Linzi*."

Linzi goes bright purple and so do I. I can't think of anything to say to her. She obviously can't think of anything to say to me, either. We sit in silence, at the tea table. I can feel her eyes on me, but every time I risk a glance she quickly swivels them away in the opposite direction, while the Microdot, for some reason best known to herself, keeps kicking at me and sticking her elbow in my ribs.

I escape as soon as I can, down to the hole to do some digging. The Herb arrives half an hour later, but Aaron, who is supposed to be joining us, fails to turn up. He is becoming very unreliable.

Me and the Herb dig for a while in silence. The Herb seems preoccupied, and I'm still brooding over the incident in the gym cupboard. It's very unnerving, having a great hefty girl walloping about on top of you, squeezing all the breath out of you. I wouldn't be at all surprised if it gives me post traumatic stress disorder.

I'm just wondering if I should unburden myself and tell the Herb about it, when quite suddenly, out of the blue, she says, "You know Sheri Stringer?"

For a minute I don't think I do, and then I remember. "Girl in your class? One with all the hair?"

The Herb says, "Yes. The one with all the hair."

"What about her?"

"Do you think she's pretty?"

Do I think Sheri Stringer is pretty? I say that I don't know. "Why?"

"Cos I'm asking you! And don't say you *don't know*. You've got to have an opinion one way or the other."

I say that I can't have an opinion as I haven't ever thought about it.

The Herb says, "So think!"

"OK." I give it a few seconds, to show that I'm thinking. What does she want me to say? Yes, or no? I have to be careful here. I don't want to upset her.

The Herb, like the Microdot, is quite an impatient sort of person. "Well, come on!" she says. "Don't take all day. Is she or isn't she?"

Cautiously, I say, "I suppose she might be… quite."

"How many marks out of ten?"

"Um… seven? Eight?"

The Herb goes, "Huh!"

Obviously I've gone and got it wrong. *Again.* Girls can be very difficult at times! Even the Herb. Trying to make amends I say that maybe seven or eight is too high. "Maybe more like… four or five. What d'you reckon?"

"No use asking *me*," says the Herb. "What's it matter

what I think?"

I tell her that it does matter. I say that I value her opinion. I ask her, does *she* think Sheri Stringer is pretty? To which she says, "Yes, I suppose... if you like sickly sweet and airbrushed." Then she hunches down and starts shovelling earth as hard as she can go, great clumps of it whizzing past my ear. I want to tell her to stop, but I can't quite summon up the courage; not the mood she's in. I dunno what the matter is. Why is she so hung up about Sheri Stringer?

To take her mind off the subject I try and interest her in the Microdot's paint splotch test, which I've brought with me, but she hardly even glances at it. Just goes on shovelling earth and every now and then giving short barks of laughter like she's really amused by something. Except I don't think she is amused.

It's all very odd, but we go on digging till almost seven o'clock, when the Herb says she's got to get back and do her homework. Aaron still hasn't put in an appearance. I wouldn't mind, except he did actually promise. He knows Dad wants his hole back by the end of the month!

When I get in, the Linzi person has gone. Mum says again that she's a real cutie, and the Microdot gives me this meaningful glare. I ignore her and go upstairs, where I find that a pink envelope has been pushed under my bedroom door. I pick it up, distastefully. I don't trust pink! Inside is a sheet of paper – more pink – with teddy bears printed on it. On the paper are the words, YOU ROCK! I tear out of my room and collar the Microdot at the top of the stairs. I wave the sheet of paper at her. I snarl, "Did you put her up to this?"

"Dunno what you're talking about," says the Microdot; and she wriggles out of my grasp and slithers off along the landing. At the door of the bathroom, she turns. "Think yourself lucky I didn't give her the number of your mobile!"

And then she sticks her tongue out and says, "I would have done, if I could remember it!" I feel like strangling her.

Thursday
I think Amy Wilkerson may have gone off me. Instead of beaming

at me she now totally ignores me; and today in maths, when she could have come and parked her bum next to me, she just sniffed, rather loudly, and went swishing past. It may have something to do with Janine Edwards and the gym cupboard, or maybe it was that thing in science the other day when Janine kept turning round and shooting these secret messages at me. I know Amy noticed cos I saw her scowling and sucking her cheeks in. I don't really know why it should bother her, but girls are quite odd that way. One minute they're the biggest best friends of all time, going round in a gaggle, all clamped together, and the next they are scratching each other's eyes out, crazed with jealousy and half insane with hatred.

Boys don't behave like that. Me and Aaron have been mates since Year 3; we don't bicker and squabble. The Microdot does! She's had about six best friends since Christmas. I just wish she'd fall out with the Linzi person, then perhaps I'd be left in peace.

Janine Edwards is my biggest worry at the moment. You'd think she'd be embarrassed, carrying on like that in the gym cupboard. Screaming her head off just because the light went out! But she's becoming very bold. She's doing the secret message thing again, flashing her eyes at me across the room whenever Mrs Duncan's back is turned. I have an uncomfortable feeling she might have tried sitting next to me if I hadn't very quickly got up and shot across to another desk, next to Stuart Wenham. Stuart gave this goofy grin and said, "That was close!"

I just don't know what the matter is with these girls. Why can't they leave me alone???

Aaron wasn't in school for the first two periods as he was at the dentist having a tooth drilled. He arrived in time for break, complaining that his lips had gone big. His lower one was all bulged out and wobbly, so he couldn't talk properly, but I had no sympathy with him. I asked him where he had been yesterday evening, when he was supposed to be helping us dig, and this shifty look came into his eyes and he mumbled, "Thorry, I frrgot." He then went on to tell me how the dentist had had to inject him twice.

"Wunth up *here*, and wunth down *here*." He said, "My nothe ith dead. I can't feel my nothe!"

I told him that it served him right. I said in future he should get his mum to make his dentist's appointments for after school.

"Otherwise I'm at their mercy!"

Aaron said, "Hoothe merthy?"

"All of 'em! Everyone! Specially Janine Edwards."

He gave this uncouth cackle and said, "Did she come an' thkwoth you again?"

I said, "It's not funny."

"I think it ith," said Aaron. "I think it'th hilariouth!"

He is supposed to be my *friend*. I told him that I hoped all his teeth would drop out.

Walked home from the bus stop with Will. He's been picking at his pimples again, but I didn't say anything as he is very self-conscious and gets easily embarrassed. I know about being embarrassed. I think Dad does, too, which is why he tries to cover up his bald patch by combing what is left of his hair over it. Mum and the Microdot, on the other hand, probably don't even know what the word means. I guess what it is, the males of this family are simply a bit more sensitive than the females. They are also less talkative. Mum and the Microdot will go rabbiting in for hours, whereas me and Will, and Dad, are more the strong silent types. Still, you have to talk about something or it gets to feel odd.

I was trying to think of a suitable topic of conversation when Will said, "So how's it going?"

I said, "Yeah, OK." Then there was a pause, and I said, "Well, apart from girls."

"Oh?" Will looked at me. He seemed surprised. "I didn't know you were into them."

I said, "I'm not."

"So what's the problem?"

"They're giving me all this hassle!" It came bursting out of me before I could stop it. I hadn't *meant* to talk to him about girls.

Will said, "What kind of hassle?"

"I dunno! Making nuisances of themselves. Always wanting to come and sit next to you, and beaming at you, and breathing over you. They just won't leave me alone! Do you have this sort of trouble?"

Will said, "I should be so lucky!"

He sounded quite violent about it. Earnestly I assured him that I didn't *invite* girls to come and breathe over me.

"They just do it. I don't know how to stop them!"

"Yeah? Like you're so irresistible?"

I said, "N-no, I – I just seem to attract them."

"Well, poor you," said Will. "My heart bleeds."

"It's giving me problems," I said.

"So go paint yourself green, or something. Go to the joke shop and buy some boils. Stick a zit on your nose. What d'you think you are? The Incredible Hunk?"

I said, "I can't understand why they keep doing it."

"Well, have I got news for you," said Will. "Neither can I!"

It seems like I upset him, though I don't know how. All I wanted was a bit of advice! I don't know who else to turn to. Aaron's my best mate, but we don't really talk about things like that. In any case, he isn't any more clued up than I am. Last time we had a conversation on the subject he told me that in his opinion girls were best kept away from. He said it was his motto in life: "Leave 'em alone cos they're no good for you!" So what help he'd be, I can't imagine. Joe and Calum aren't much better. Their idea of a conversation about girls is a series of Neanderthal grunts and sniggers.

I suppose I could try the Herb. I mean, she's a girl, sort of. What I mean, she *is* a girl; just not like other girls. Least, not the ones I know. Still, she probably understands them better than me or Aaron. I think I might ask her. I can't carry on like this! I need some kind of help.

While we were having tea, Wee Scots and Mum started up a discussion about this girl they'd seen on television that they thought was disgusting. Mum said she was "shameless" 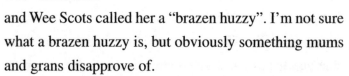 and Wee Scots called her a "brazen huzzy". I'm not sure what a brazen huzzy is, but obviously something mums and grans disapprove of.

Mum said, "So *ugly*. Why do they have to make themselves so *ugly*?" And then she turned to Will and said, "I suppose you thought she was attractive?"

Will gave this kind of hollow laugh, like "ha ha" without any gurgle. "Why ask me?" he said. "Ask the Hunk over there. He's the expert."

The Microdot did the curling thing with her lip. She said, "*Him?* He doesn't know the first thing! He doesn't even *like* girls."

"Guess that's why they're all after him," said Will.

"Och, no!" said Wee Scots. "I'd fancy him myself if I were a few years younger. He's grown into a right wee hunk!"

Dad cried, "Hunky Dory!" and he and Mum, and Wee Scots, all laughed, like Dad had said something really funny.

Afterwards, while we were doing the washing up, the Microdot said, "That was so clever! Calling you Hunky Dory."

I said, "Why? What's clever about it?"

"Well," she said, "hunky dory… it's an *expression*, stupid! Don't tell me you've never heard it? You've never heard *hunky dory*? I thought everyone had heard it!"

I said, "Well, I haven't, so what's it mean?"

"Means, like, OK. Everything is hunky dory. Not," she added, "that *I* think you're particularly hunky. But Linzi does. And you just treat her *so badly*. I can't think what she sees in you! I can't think what any of them see in you. It's not just cos you're my brother, it's cos of all these really nerdy things you do, like going off and digging your stupid hole instead of talking to Linzi. That was just *so* nerdy. It's what Dad should have called you... not Hunky Dory. Nerdy Dory! Rather dig holes than talk to a *girl*."

This is exactly what I mean about going on. She kept at it the whole time we're washing up. On, and on, and on. Last thing she said, as we left the kitchen, "I still can't *believe* you didn't know what hunky dory means! I know what it means, and I'm only ten years old. How come I know, and not you?"

So she knew and I didn't. So what??? I know all kinds of things that she doesn't! She doesn't know that the biggest dinosaur was called an Argentinosaurus and was as tall as a six-storey building. She doesn't know that the very first dinosaurs lived 230 million years ago. She doesn't know that back in those days all the continents we have now were one huge great supercontinent called Pangea. I bet she's never even heard of Pangea!

She has absolutely *nothing* to boast about. She couldn't even tell the difference between a stegosaurus and a triceratops.

I've noticed that most girls aren't really very interested in dinosaurs; not even the Herb. It's strange. I can't understand it.

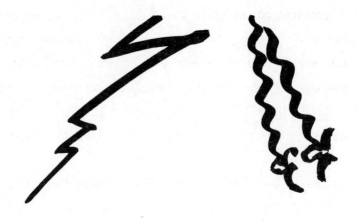

five

Sunday

She said, *"Doodle!"* and thrust a pencil and a sheet of paper at me. I really don't know why I let her keep bullying me like this. It's a kind of blackmail. If I don't do what she wants she'll say I've got something to hide, and accuse me of being mad, and weird, and anti-social. Except that she accuses me of that anyway! It's very demeaning, being dictated to by a ten year old. I wish now that I'd told her to go and chuck herself out with the rubbish.

"Well, go on!" she said. "Don't think about it, just *doodle*."

I tried to do something strong and manly, to show her that I wasn't intimidated by her and her nonsense, but it's very difficult when someone tells you to just doodle; you can never be sure what's going to come out.

"Let's have a look!" She snatched the paper away and sat there, frowning. "Hm," she said, at last. "Very interesting."

I said, "So what's it show? Does it show I'm going to come sleepwalking into your room one night and smother you with a pillow?"

She put her head on one side, considering. "Is that what *you* think it shows?"

I said, "Don't ask me! You're supposed to be the expert."

She liked that; me calling her the expert.

"I shall have to study it," she said. "It's not that easy. After all, I'm only ten years old. I'm still learning!"

"Yeah," I said, "I noticed."

"Don't worry, I'll work at it! I'll find out for you."

"Can't wait," I muttered.

"Would you like to know what Linzi's showed?"

I said, "No, thank you very much." But she told me anyway.

91

"Showed she's really suffering. All because of you! I don't know *why* you're so against girls."

I tried to protest that I wasn't, but before I could say anything the Microdot had gone rushing on.

"Your friend Aaron likes them OK. I saw him the other night with Sophy Timms."

I said, "Aaron and Sophy Timms? You've gotta be joking!"

"I'm not joking, I saw them… coming out the park. That night Linzi was here and you were so horrible to her. Night you went and dug your hole."

The night Aaron was supposed to come and help and didn't turn up. But Aaron wouldn't go out with Sophy Timms! He wouldn't go out with any girl. He was the one who said girls were no good for you. Best kept away from.

"It was when we were taking Linzi back, we drove past the park, and I saw them. We both saw them. They were holding hands. It really upset poor Linzi! I mean, considering you won't even *talk* to her. And there's your best friend actually *holding hands*?"

"Must have been someone else," I said. "Can't have been Aaron."

"It was, too! Ask him, if you don't believe me. *He's* not against girls!"

I really resent that. I'm not against girls! I just don't like it when they get silly. Boys don't get silly. Me and Aaron wouldn't go and sit next to a girl and start breathing over her, and beaming at her, and treading on her foot underneath the desk. I don't care what the Microdot says! Aaron wouldn't go out with Sophy Timms.

"What is so *odd*," said the Microdot, "you don't seem to object to the Herb."

I said, "That's different. The Herb's all right… she's as good as a boy."

I knew at once that I'd said the wrong thing. The Microdot's eyes narrowed to slits. She can look really mean when she narrows her eyes.

"Say that again?" she said.

"Say what again?"

"What you just said! About the Herb."

"Said she's as good as a boy," I mumbled.

"You sexist **PIG**!"

I sidestepped, nervously, before she could swipe me. "I didn't mean anything by it! I just meant… she doesn't get silly like other girls."

"*Silly?*" said the Microdot. "*SILLY?*" she shrieked.

"Like – you know! Giggling, and – breathing, and—"

"So now we're not supposed to *breathe*?"

"Over people. Breathing *over* people."

"What people?"

"Well – boys," I said. "Girls coming and breathing over boys."

Now she was staring at me like I was some kind of lunatic. "You've been *breathed* over?"

I said, "Yes. I have."

"By a *girl*?"

"Yes."

"Oh, wow!" The Microdot clutched at herself in mock horror. "What a terrible experience! How did you survive? He was *breathed* over!"

"It wasn't funny," I said.

"No," shrieked the Microdot, "and neither are you! You are just so antisocial it's unbelievable. You ought to have an abso put on you!"

"*Asbo*," I said. "The word is *asbo*. Antisocial behaviour order."

"I know what it means!" screeched the Microdot.

"It's for people that go round causing vandalism."

"You cause vandalism! You wreck people's lives! Poor Linzi can't hardly *eat* because of you. She'll fade away to nothing, and it'll be all your fault. You hate her so much you can't even be bothered to talk to her!"

I said, "I told you before, I don't hate her, I just don't

want to encourage her. I think that would be very unkind," I said, "cos there isn't any future. And if you were really her friend you'd tell her so!"

The Microdot ignored this. She always ignores things she doesn't like or can't answer. I've noticed it before, it's a ploy of hers. It's very dishonest; she's like a politician.

"I'm going to go now," she said, "and work out what this doodle means. When I've worked it out'" – she looked at me, coldly – "I'll let you know."

Like I said, I can't wait.

Monday
Got hold of Aaron at school this morning and told him what the Microdot had said.

"Said she saw you coming out the park with Sophy Timms... said you was holding hands."

Aaron's face turned a strange mottled colour. Sort of pink and white, in patches. I could see that I'd seriously embarrassed him. That anyone could think, even for a moment, that he would hold hands with Sophy Timms! I felt sorry I'd ever brought it up.

"That Microdot," I said. "I told her it couldn't be you!"

"Yeah. Well. Thing is—" Aaron swallowed. I saw his Adam's apple bob up and down like a ping-pong ball. He's got a very scrawny neck, has Aaron. "Thing is, I did sort of go up the park with her. Helped her take her dog for a walk. It's a very big dog. Very strong. Like a cross between a German Shepherd and a Pyrenean mountain dog. Weighs more 'n she does. I was just kind of helping her, like, control it, sort of thing. Cos she lives in our road, right? Just a few doors away. So when she asks me, could I go with her cos she's scared the dog might pull her over, I'm, like, what can I do? How can I get out of it? Not wanting to be rude, or anything."

"Could've said you were s'pposed to be coming and helping me dig."

"Yeah. That's right! I could've. Dunno why I didn't, really. 'Cept... well! Fact is—" He swallowed again. I

96

saw his Adam's apple almost bounce right out of his throat. "I'm sort of, like, kind of going out with her!"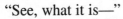

What??? There's this long silence. I'm in a state of shock. Totally gobsmacked.

"See, what it is—"

Aaron? My best mate? Going out with a *girl*?

"What it is—"

Aaron, *holding hands*?

"I'm in training!" he says.

I still can't get my head round it.

"Training to be a giggle-o!"

I pull myself together and say, "What's a giggle-o?" I've never heard of a giggle-o. Aaron says it's a man that's looked after by an older woman. I think about it.

"You mean, like a mum?"

He says no, like a girlfriend. "'Cept older. They keep you, so's you don't have to bother going out to work. I read about it in this magazine at the dentist. Reckoned it sounded like a good idea. I mean, just staying at home watching telly or playing on the computer. You know?"

He looked at me, hopefully. "Gotta be better than dragging off out to some boring office every day. Just gotta find the right girl."

I say, "A girl that's older."

"Yeah, yeah! They've gotta be older."

I point out that Sophy Timms is the same age as we are.

"Nah!" Aaron shakes his head, excitedly. "She's twelve already!"

I say, "That counts as *older*?"

"Well, a few months," says Aaron. "Gotta start somewhere! Like I said, I'm in training. But it's all right, I don't have to train every day. I'll see if I can take a bit of time off, come round and do some digging for you."

I find this all very disturbing. Why can't things just stay the same as they've always been? Life is suddenly full of worrying complications. I can't believe that Aaron would desert me and the Herb for Sophy Timms! But it's not just Aaron, it's life in general. It's *girls* in particular.

Thursday
Sheri Stringer came up to me today. (She's the one with all the hair. It's quite frightening, it springs about all

over her head like forked lightning. Some kind of secret weapon…get spiked by the hair and psszzzz! Fried to a crisp.) Anyway, she kind of sidles up to me when I'm all by myself in the corridor and says, "Hi, Dory!" I go, "Yeah, hi."

She asks what class I'm going to, and I say maths, to which she says, "Yuck!" I say that I actually don't mind maths, what class has she got? She says she's got PE, so now it's me going yuck. But I'm hoping she'll peel off towards the sports hall and leave me alone, cos I don't like the way she's doing that flappy thing with her eyelashes. Flip, flap. How do they *do* that?

We pass the turn off for the sports hall. I stop and say, "I thought you had PE?"

She says, "Yes. It's so gruesome! Do you like the Voice of Man?"

For a minute I can't think what she's talking about, and then I remember it's this band that Will likes and the Microdot doesn't cos she says it's sexist. Anything with the word man in it is sexist, according to the Microdot. She tries to have arguments with Will about it, but he's too mature to have arguments with a ten year old. I wish I could be that mature!

Sheri's still waiting for an answer, so I just kind of mumble at her.

"I've got their latest album," she says. "Wanna come round some time and hear it?"

I say no, that's OK, my brother's a fan, he's bound to have it.

"It'd sound better at my place," she says.

Why? Why does she say that? It would sound exactly the same! It doesn't make any sense.

"Well, think about it," she says. "See ya!"

I say, "Yeah, see ya."

Sheri goes off in the direction of the sports hall and I carry on down the corridor, where I find Aaron waiting for me outside the maths room. He has this idiotic grin on his face.

"Saw who you were talking to," he says.

I grunt. A grunt is supposed to discourage. It's sign language for *drop it*. But Aaron's never been one for observing the social niceties (as Big Nan calls them). He's practically jumping up and down on the spot.

"So what'd she want? Want you to go out with her? Are you going to?"

I say, "No, she didn't, and no I'm not."

"Could do a lot worse," says Aaron. "I mean, Sheri Stringer…" He pulls a face and starts making animal noises. I tell him to shut up.

"She just wanted me to go round her place and listen to a CD."

"Oh, yeah?" says Aaron. "Oh, yeah?"

"Yeah!"

I give him a shove and we jostle together into the maths room and head for our usual seats. As we sit down, Aaron leans over and whispers hoarsely in my ear.

"Reckon you're on to a good thing there… she obviously fancies you!"

He says that about everyone. I'm learning not to pay too much attention to Aaron. I really don't think he knows what he's talking about.

He came round this evening to do some digging. He said he could only stay half an hour as he had to go and help Sophy Timms take her dog out again. He explained to the Herb how it was a very big dog.

"Half bulldog and half German Shepherd."

"I thought you said half Pyrenean mountain dog?" I said.

"Yeah, well. Whatever."

"He still has to help her take it out," said the Herb. "Cos she's so pathetic and weak she can't manage it herself."

"It's a very strong dog," said Aaron. "Almost as big as she is."

"Then she ought to have got a tiny *little* dog to go with her tiny little self. A little tiny *lap* dog," said the Herb.

"She didn't choose it," said Aaron. "It's her mum's."

"Then why doesn't her mum take it out?"

Aaron said, "I dunno."

I was about to tell the Herb that the dog thing was just a ploy. "He's training to be a giggle-o." But before I could say it, Aaron had gone bundling on again.

"Know Sheri Stringer?" he said. "That girl in your class? I reckon she fancies old Dory!"

"*Oh?*" The Herb stopped digging and gave me this

look. This *look*. I don't know what it is about girls. If they're not flapping their eyelashes – which the Herb would never do – they're *shrivelling* you.

I told Aaron to be quiet and get on with his digging.

"We've only got another few days. I haven't found as much as a trilobite!"

"Would you expect to find as much as a trilobite?" said the Herb.

I said, "Well, you never know. I mean, they do turn up."

"What, in Warrington Crescent?"

"Why not?"

There was this kind of pause; then very politely the Herb said, "What exactly *is* a trilobite?"

Aaron let out a howl. "Don't ask, don't ask!"

"I just wanted to know," said the Herb. "In case we came across one."

Aaron groaned. Determinedly, I took no notice. (Following my new rule.) I like it when the Herb shows an interest. I told her how trilobites had lived 300 million years ago, and had gone extinct before the dinosaurs had even come into existence. I added the bit about the dinosaurs so that she could understand just how long ago it really was. It is sometimes difficult for people, if they are not used to thinking in terms of millions. I told her how they were sea creatures; bottom dwellers. Aaron immediately shouted, "*Bottom dwellers?*"

I ignored him.

"They lived in shallow water, and fed on d—"

"Stuff out of bottoms!"

"*Detritus*," I said.

"Breakfast?" said Aaron.

"Do you mind?" said the Herb. "I'm trying to learn something here. Go on, Deeje! What did they look like? How big were they?"

I told her that they were all different sizes. How the average was probably somewhere between about three centimetres and ten, but the biggest one that had ever been found was nearer seventy.

"*Seventy centimetres!* Can you imagine? That's amazing, for a trilobite."

Aaron said, "Yeah, wouldn't want a thing that big coming at you."

"Don't be such a wimp!" The Herb turned, and whacked at him with her trowel. "Let's get digging! See if we can find some."

I do love the Herb! She is one of my favourite people. She may even be my *most* favourite people. Person. I just wish Aaron hadn't gone and told her about Sheri Stringer. I don't know why he had to do that.

At five o'clock he went off to help Sophy Timms exercise her mum's vast enormous dog. "It's way too big for her to cope on her own."

"Yes, cos she is *so* tiny," said the Herb.

"This is it! Could pull her over."

"Oh, screech!" The Herb fell down, dramatically, at the bottom of the hole.

"'S all right for you," said Aaron, as he climbed out. "You're more like a boy."

The Herb scrambled back to her feet. She made a rude gesture with a finger. Then she said a rude word. Her language can be quite bad sometimes.

"Hey, Deeje," she said. "Who's this?" She clasped both hands to her chest. "Poor lickle *me*! I'm tho *thmall*, I'm tho *tiny*, I need a big thtwong boy to help me. Oh, oh, thith twowel ith *tho-o-o* heavy, I can't hold it!"

I said, "Yeah, that does sound a bit like her."

"Sounds *exactly* like her. We call her Barbie, like Barbie doll. Did you know she wears knickers with little pink flowers on them?"

I shook my head. I wasn't sure it was something I wanted to know.

"*Pink!*" said the Herb. "I can't stand pink. Can you?"

"It's a bit girly," I said.

"Course, some boys like girls that are girly. They like it when they squeak and twitter and say they can't do things. It's what some boys want. It makes them feel macho." The Herb picked up a sieveful of earth and started shaking it, vigorously. "Does it make you feel macho?"

"M-me?" I said. "N-no!"

"You can say if it does."

"It doesn't," I said.

The Herb went on shaking. "I won't laugh at you. I know you can't help it, it's just the way boys are."

I said, "I'm not!"

"You don't have to feel *guilty*. It's a hormone thing, it – oooh, look!" She suddenly thrust the sieve under my nose. "Is that a trilobite?"

Unfortunately it wasn't, but at least the Herb tries, which is more than Aaron does. I've felt for the last few days that his mind hasn't really been on his work. Now I know the reason why: *Sophy Timms*.

I just would never have thought it.

Friday

I meant to tell the Herb, yesterday, about Aaron training to be a giggle-o, but what with one thing and another, mainly a Russell managing to wriggle its way under the wire netting and get into the hole, then all the others starting to yammer and squabble, and the one that got in doing its best to dig down to Australia before I could grab hold of it – well, what with all that going on I never got around to it. Now I am very glad that I didn't.

Over tea this evening the Microdot said, "Did you ask him?"

I said, "Who?"

"Aaron!"

"Did I ask him what?"

"If he's going out with Sophy Timms!"

"Oh, that! Yeah. I asked him," I said.

"So is he?"

"Yeah. Sort of."

"You mean, *he's* got a girlfriend!"

"Well, no, not really," I said. "She's not really a girlfriend. What it is, he's training to become a giggle-o."

I thought that would impress her! She didn't know what it meant. Dad obviously did, cos he choked into his tea and said, "Training to become a *what*?"

"Giggle-o," I said. And for the benefit of the Microdot I added, "It's someone that gets looked after by an older woman."

The Microdot shrieked, "Sophy Timms isn't an older woman!"

"I told you," I said, "he's training. Gotta start somewhere."

It was at this point I became aware that the rest of the table – Mum, Dad, Will, Wee Scots – were all convulsed and spluttering.

"What's funny?" I said.

Will gasped. "It's not giggle-o, it's jiggle-o! G-i-g-o-l-o. *Jiggle-o!*"

At which they all fell about, including the Microdot.

"Jiggle-o, jiggle-o!"

It was extremely humiliating; I should have known better than to quote Aaron. He was the one that confused pederast with Prendergast. He was also the one that thought medieval was spelled middle evil. Now he has gone and made me look stupid in front of the Microdot. I am quite angry; I intend to speak to him about it. He is definitely not to be relied upon.

The Microdot has just pounded on my bedroom door and yelled at me to let her in.

I said, "What d'you want? I'm busy."

She said, "I've worked out what your doodle means. Let me in and I'll tell you!"

I said, "I'm not sure I wanna to be told… not if all you're going to do is say I'm a weirdo."

"I'm not, I'm not!" She shoved herself past me and bounced down on to my beanbag, scattering three of the Russells who had been lying there quite peacefully, for once.

I said, "Go on, then! Tell me – and don't take all day about it. I've got things to do."

"Right! Well. OK. What it means… it means you'd really like to go out with Linzi, but you're too scared to ask her!"

I said, "What a load of total rubbish!"

Earnestly she assured me that it was not rubbish. "You can tell a lot about someone from the way they doodle. See, look, this line *here*, sort of leaping forward… that's you, right? And this bit *here*, this is Linzi – see? Where you've drawn plaits? That's Linzi."

I said, "What d'you mean, *plaits*? It's not plaits, it's just lines!"

110

"That's how it seems to you," said the Microdot. "But deep down in your sub-conscious, it's plaits. You didn't *know* you were drawing plaits—"

"Yeah, cos I wasn't."

"You were! You just didn't know it. That's why it's called your sub-conscious. Cos you're not *conscious*. OK?"

I shook my head. There is absolutely no point in arguing with her.

I said, "Yeah, clear as mud."

She looked at me, reproachfully. "I thought you'd be pleased."

Why? What's to be pleased about?

"Even when I try to be nice to you, you're rude and ungrateful!"

I said, "How was I rude?"

"Saying it was crap!"

"Pardon me," I said, "but that was you. I just said it was rubbish."

"It's still rude and ungrateful! I don't know why I bother."

"Feel free not to," I said, as she flounced out the door.

"I've got to. I can't stop *now*. I'm doing your profile!"

"Did I ask you to?"

She turned, and smiled, very sweetly. "No, but if you don't co-operate I'll know you've got something to hide!"

It's frightening. If she's like this when she's ten, what's she going to be like when she's my age?

six

Sunday

Another of her stupid tests.

"Draw faces!" she said.

So I drew faces. Six of 'em, cos that's what she told me to do. I made them all happy and smiling. I knew if I made them miserable, she'd have a go at me; I thought I'd get good marks for drawing smileys. Instead, she took one look and said, "Why are they all *happy*?" She said nobody draws six faces all happy. "It's not normal!"

"'Tis for me," I said.

"Then *you're* not normal! Just shows you've got something to hide. You thought if you drew six happy faces you could trick me, but you can't, you see, cos it's too obvious. Normal people draw a *mixture*. cos nobody's happy all the time."

"This is such a load of crap," I said.

"You keep saying that!" She crowed, triumphantly. "It just proves that I'm right… when someone doesn't like what they discover about themselves they say it's crap, and if you use that word again I shall tell Mum!"

"Know what?" I said. "You're a real creep!"

"Yes, and you're a total plonk!"

Whatever that means. I don't know why I let her get to me like this, I really don't. She's gone off now, all self-important, to work on my profile; I've come upstairs to brood. I do brood. I get very anxious and depressed and wonder what is wrong with me and why I can't be the same as other people. Most of the time I'm quite happy just being me, but then the Microdot starts on and I lose all my confidence. She is always so sure of herself! Why can't I be sure of myself?

I am feeling quite low. I shall have to make a list.

List of Dinosaur Objects in my Bedroom

Two pterodactyls flying up the wall

A model of a stegosaurus

114

A triceratops poster

An inflatable tyrannosaurus (95 cm. tall)

A basket full of dinosaur eggs (not real ones, but they look real)

A giant pteranodon suspended from the ceiling

12 mini dinosaurs on a shelf above my bed

A small woolly mammoth (which of course is not an actual dinosaur, merely a prehistoric mammal, but Wee Scots gave it to me for my fifth birthday and it kind of fits in with the general theme)

I also have:

All my dinosaur books (listed previously)

2 dinosaur DVDs

+ a DVD of Jurassic Park.

Oh, and also my collection of trilobites which Dad bought for me off e-bay. One of the best presents I have ever had!

Mum says that entering my room is like going into a cave in the Jurassic period. She says Jurassic as that is the only one she has heard of. Actually it is a mixture of Triassic, Jurassic and Cretaceous, but I doubt if Mum would pay much attention if I tried telling her this. Even the Herb goes a bit glazed when I start talking about

things that took place millions of years ago. I suppose it is more than your average person can cope with.

I am feeling a bit better, now. More in control. Making lists restores order to my life. I cannot live haphazardly, like the Microdot! She simply has no sense of direction. Neither has Mum. It is always me that does the map reading in the car, even if Will is there. He

is good, but I am even better. I am the champion!

Tomorrow I intend to have a stern word with Aaron on the subject of *giggle-o-s*.

Monday

Had a long talk with Aaron. Told him how he'd made me look like an idiot in front of my whole family.

"The word happens to be *jiggle-o*," I said. "Not *giggle-o*."

He argued, same as he always does. You can't tell Aaron anything, he always knows best. Thinks he knows best.

"Who says it's jiggle-o?"

"My brother."

"Not that stupid Microdot? Cos if it's her, she doesn't know what she's talking about."

"It wasn't her! I just said, it was Will."

"Yeah? Well, I've *seen* the word, I know how it's spelt. It's spelt giggle-o."

I said, "It may be spelt giggle-o, but that's not the way it's said."

Even then he had to challenge me. "How do *you* know? You'd never even heard it before you got it off me!"

I said, "I know cos I'm capable of learning. I listen when people tell me things. I don't just go arguing on!"

I might as well have saved my breath, all the notice he took.

"G-I-G! Like what people do in clubs... they do *gigs*. Yeah? *Gigs*. Not *jigs*. You ever heard of anyone going to a jig? Course you haven't, cos they don't! They go to gigs. G-I-G... *gig*."

I didn't know what to say to that. In the end I told him to just shut up and accept that he was wrong.

"Same like you always are. Like you were with Prendergast. You're just not reliable," I said. "Like oh, yes, I'll be round to help you dig, no problem! I'll be there. And then you go off helping someone walk their dog and don't even bother telling me."

"I did tell you!"

"*Afterwards.* Not much point telling someone *afterwards.*"

"Yeah, well, I'll be helping her again this evening," said Aaran. "And I'm telling you now, so's you'll know."

I said, "Must get a lot of exercise, that dog."

"Needs it," said Aaron. "It's a big dog. Cross between a wolfhound and a Great Dane."

So far it's been a cross between about six different breeds. German Shepherd, Pyrenean mountain dog, bulldog, St Bernard… it's probably a Yorkshire terrier.

"Guess I'd better tell the Herb you're not coming," I said.

Aaron said, "Yeah, an' while you're about it you can tell her I don't want her bashing me no more!"

I couldn't remember that she ever had bashed him, but he reminded me that last time he had come to help dig she had hit him on the head with her trowel.

"And she swore. It's not right, girls swearing. She's not very fem'nine," said Aaron. "I wouldn't go and help *her* with her dog!"

"She wouldn't need you to," I said. "She could manage by herself."

"Yeah, being all butch and belligerent," said Aaron.

I wasn't sure that I liked him calling the Herb butch and belligerent. I mean, she *is* – but so what?

"Sophy's more like a reg'lar girl."

"Like a Barbie doll," I said.

It was at that point the bell rang and we had to go into class, which was probably just as well. I'd hate to quarrel with my best mate over anything as silly as a *girl*.

I just read through what I wrote. I didn't actually mean that girls are silly, just that it would be silly to quarrel over them. That's all.

The Herb came round after tea wearing her boiler suit, all ready to dig. I told her that Aaron wouldn't be coming. She said, "I s'ppose he's helping the tiny little helpless dwarf thing walk her massive great dog that she can't manage on account of being so *flimsy*."

I said, "Yeah. I dunno what he sees in her. He's gone all macho and protective."

"Pathetic!"

"It is," I said. "It is pathetic."

"Hope you don't ever get like that."

I said, "Me? No way!"

"You'd better not," said the Herb.

"I won't!"

There was a bit of a silence then she said, "So we gonna dig, or what?"

"Maybe we ought to go up the park," I said. "Take Polly and Jack."

"But what about the hole?"

I told her that one night off wouldn't hurt. She seemed surprised. I was a bit surprised, myself. Why would I want to go up the park when there was serious digging to be done? I mumbled that Mum hadn't been able to give the dogs a good walk this morning, which was absolutely not true, as Mum always gives the dogs a good walk, but I had to have some excuse. You can't just go up the park for no reason.

The Herb suggested we take all of them, but I drew the line at that. Five Jack Russells can drive a person mad. A normal person, that is. I said that we would just take Polly and Jack, as they are the youngest. So that is what we did.

The first thing we saw as we entered the park was Aaron and Sophy Timms, walking round the path on the far side. They were holding hands.

"Eurgh, yuck, look at that!" The Herb minced, doing

her Barbie doll thing. "Look what it's wearing!"

I couldn't really see, from that distance; not in any detail. It just looked like ordinary sort of stuff to me, the sort of stuff that most girls wear, but then I am not an expert in these matters. It is probably true to say that I know more about the mating habits of dinosaurs than about girls' clothes.

"*Pink*," said the Herb.

"Oh. Yeah! Right." I nodded. Pink was puke; even I knew that.

"Looks like a bunch of candyfloss… catch me wearing pink! And where's the great enormous dog?"

There wasn't any dog. I mean, she's probably got one, somewhere, but it certainly wasn't there this evening. The dog was just a ploy, to get Aaron out of digging. He'd sooner come up the park and hold hands! What did he get out of it, just walking round the park?

"He's gone totally soppy," said the Herb. She minced again, flapping her arms and doing little twizzles.

"Skippity hoppity! Look at *me!*"

He obviously got something out of it. I wondered what would happen if I held the Herb's hand. I almost got brave and gave it a go, but before I could quite bring myself to do it she'd gone twirling off across the grass with Jack and Polly snapping at her heels. Probably just as well. I felt somewhat shaken and was glad we had brought the dogs with us as it gave me the opportunity to exercise a bit of authority.

"JACK! POLLY! COME BACK HERE!"

Not that they took any notice, but it was a manly sort of shout.

"I enjoyed that," said the Herb, when we'd been right round the park and arrived back at the gates. Jack had found a punctured football and he and the Herb had played with it all across the grass. Polly had mainly just made a nuisance of herself, while I had walked sternly on along the path, brooding about Aaron and wondering what it all meant.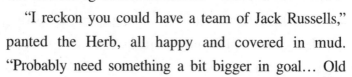

"I reckon you could have a team of Jack Russells," panted the Herb, all happy and covered in mud. "Probably need something a bit bigger in goal... Old

English Sheepdog, or something. Hey!" She nudged me. "You coming to see me play footie on Thursday?"

I said, "You bet!"

"It's after school."

"That's OK."

"It'll mean you miss out on digging again."

"Doesn't matter."

"But you've only got another two weeks. Aaron ought to be helping! He's your best mate."

I said, "Yeah. Well—"

"I suppose he thinks she's *pretty*?"

"What, the Barbie doll?" I looked at her in assembly the other day, and it seemed to me that she might be, but I'm not sure that I can trust my judgement; not when it comes to girls. I haven't studied them like I've studied dinosaurs. "Do you think she's pretty?"

"Me?" The Herb gave this short bark of laughter, like *Huh!* "I suppose some people might think she is… if that's what they go for. All flimsy and feeble."

I can see what she means; sort of. I can't imagine Sophy Timms ever coming to help dig. She'd be too worried about getting her clothes messed up, or breaking her fingernails, or being rained on. If I ever have a girlfriend I wouldn't want one that's scared of a bit of mud.

Tuesday

Bumped into the Microdot, coming out of school. She was lurking, at the gates. *Not on her own.* In this loud, trumpeting voice she went, "YOU REMEMBER MY FRIEND LINZI, DON'T YOU?"

I said, "Oh. Yeah. Right! Hi," and shot down the road towards the bus stop, followed by the pair of them, both giggling. The Microdot later explained that "Linzi wasn't giggling cos she thinks you're funny, she was giggling cos that's how it gets her, having this thing about you. She thinks you are just *sooo* Hunky Dory!" And, "Oh, look!" she squealed. "He's gone all red! I've embarrassed him!"

I should think anyone would be embarrassed, being shrieked at by the Microdot in the middle of the street.

"Just button it," I said.

She pouted. "You are *so* repressed, it's just not true! There's poor Linzi, pining away to practically nothing, and all you can say is *button it.* You'll be sorry when she goes into a decline!"

I said, "She'll get over it. She's only ten."

"That is the most insulting remark I ever heard!" shrieked the Microdot. "You're not just a *sexist* pig, you pig, you're an ageist one, as well!"

I deny that I am sexist. *Or* ageist. Maybe I shouldn't

126

have said that about being only ten, since being ten doesn't mean you can't have feelings. I remember being ten myself and being seriously wounded by the way my family persistently made fun of me and of my ambitions, like their "Dory and his dinosaurs" jokes. It was very hurtful. I certainly don't want to hurt anyone, that is the last thing I want to do, but she just gets me so mad! The Microdot, that is. I don't blame her friend. I daresay she can't help it and anyway it's my totally irritating sister that eggs her on. Left to herself she would probably be a perfectly harmless sort of person that wouldn't dream of going round giggling at people and upsetting them.

Did some digging on my own. The Herb had football practice and Aaron was out hand-holding again. Didn't uncover anything; couldn't seem to get as enthusiastic as usual. Dunno why. Kept thinking about going up the park with the Herb. It is all very unsettling.

Wednesday

Had a very odd dream last night. I was down in a tomb, rescuing the Herb from a horde of beetles. I know what it was, it was that stupid conversation I had with the Microdot about *The Mummy* film and me looking like Brendan Fraser. In my dream I was acting like Brendan Fraser! I'd picked up the Herb and was rushing her to safety, pursued by all these rampaging beetles. It was quite exciting, but sort of weird at the same time. The Herb didn't look like the Herb, she looked more like some sort of Ancient Egyptian. Like Cleopatra, or someone. But I knew that it *was* the Herb.

It's a bit disturbing, really. I can understand being chased by beetles, but why did the Herb look like Cleopatra? And what was she doing in my dream, anyway? Specially dressed in all that floaty type stuff. The Herb wouldn't be seen dead in stuff like that! I can't begin to make any sense of it. It is a puzzle.

Thursday

Stayed on after school to watch the football. Some boys I know jeer at the thought of girls playing football, but I am not one of them. I reckon girls can do whatever they want. I'm cool about it! I used to think Aaron was, too, but just lately I'm not so sure. He has definitely changed. I told him that the Herb was the only Year 7 girl on the team, thinking he would be impressed, but all he said was, "Most girls wouldn't want to be on the team."

This annoyed me quite considerably. I said, "Why wouldn't they?"

"Look at it this way," said Aaron. "Would you wanna be on a netball team?"

I said I wouldn't want to be on any team, but if I had to be on one then netball might well be the one I'd choose.

"You're only saying that," said Aaron. "Netball's a girls' game! There's girls' games and there's boys' games, and football's a boys' game."

I asked him how he knew this. "Is there some kind of law about it?"

He said, "It's just one of those things. Stands to reason! All that kicking and barging and falling about in the mud… what sort of girl would want to do that?"

I said, "Probably not the sort of girl that needs help taking her dog out." I nearly said, her *imaginary* dog, but didn't want to get into complications. Even as it was, he got a bit offended. He said that all he was saying was kicking and barging and falling about in the mud wasn't what he personally would call a very feminine kind of thing to do. He added that of course the Herb wasn't a very feminine kind of person.

"I just hope you told her not to bash me any more!"

I said, "No, I didn't. If she wants to bash you, she can bash you, far as I'm concerned."

Aaron said, "That's encouraging violence, that is."

I opened my mouth to say, "So what?" but before I could get the words out a great cheer went up and we realised that we had missed a goal.

"Who got it?" said Aaron. "Was it the Herb? She'll do her nut if we tell her we didn't see it! She'll bash me again for sure. Hey!" He poked a finger at a girl that was standing nearby. "Who scored?"

"We did," said the girl.

"Yeah, but who got it?"

She giggled and said, "Who d'you think?"

We both turned and looked at the pitch. We couldn't see the Herb for all the kissing and hugging that was going on, so then we knew: she had scored a goal and

we hadn't seen it.

"Whatever you do," said Aaron, earnestly, "don't tell her!"

The girl giggled again, and I suddenly recognised her as the Herb's little gnome-like friend, Lottie. I call her gnome-like as she looks exactly like one of the gnomes which our next door neighbour has in her back garden. She has a whole colony of gnomes. Fishing gnomes and smoking gnomes, and beaming gnomes and sitting gnomes. The Herb's friend looks like one of the beaming ones. She beamed at us

now and promised that she wouldn't breathe a word.

"Did she really bash you?" she asked Aaron.

Aaron said, "Yeah, with a trowel. Right here." He tapped the side of his head. "Left a mark."

"It was his own fault," I said. "He was messing around instead of getting on with things. See, we're digging this hole—"

Lottie said, "I know. I've heard about it from the Herb."

I was pleased at that. I'm glad the Herb talks about our hole. It shows that she cares. *Unlike Aaron*. I turned, sternly, to look at him.

"There's only another couple of weeks to go," I said, "before Dad wants his bit of garden back."

Aaron said, "Yeah, all right, all right! Don't keep on, watch the football! I'll see if I can get round tomorrow. No! Saturday. No! Monday. Best make it Monday. I'll come round Monday. After I've helped walk Zookie Boy."

I said, "*Zookie* Boy?"

"Sophy's dog."

Lottie giggled.

"She can't manage on her own," said Aaron. "I have to go with her."

I said, "Yeah, it's a massive great dog… cross between a Yorkshire terrier and a Pekingese. What's wrong with Friday or Saturday?"

"Going to the dentist."

"What, both days?"

"Friday. I might have to have fillings. Don't wanna come an' dig if I've had fillings."

"So what about Saturday?"

"Nah, got things to do on Saturday."

I said, "Like what?"

"Just things. Don't worry, I'll be round Monday. Tell the Herb, and we'll have a mass dig."

"Would you like me to come, as well?" said Lottie. "I could dig! If there's room, that is."

I assured her that there would be. "It's a really big hole!"

She is going to come with the Herb, after school on Monday. She seems like a really sensible, intelligent sort of girl, obviously eager to learn. I think she will be a valuable addition to the team. I'm still worried about Aaron, though. Since when did him or me have things to do that we don't tell each other about?

Friday

Came home on the bus this afternoon with the Herb. Told her about Aaron going off and "doing things". She said, "Yes, I know, he's going with the Barbie Doll to see a dance show."

I said, "*Dance* show? *Aaron?*"

"She's been boasting about it all morning, how her mum had got tickets."

"A *dance* show?" I'm not surprised he didn't tell me. Not that I have anything against people dancing; I don't have anything against anything. Live and let live is what Wee Scots always says, and I agree with her. But

Aaron? The mind boggles. It's still boggling. I can hardly believe it!

"Want me to come round and help dig?" said the Herb, as we got off the bus.

I said no, it was OK, she'd done her fair share. "How about we go up the park again?"

I don't know why I said that. I certainly didn't mean to say it. It just came out before I could stop it. I'm losing control of my voice!

The Herb giggled and said, "*Again?*"

I said, "Yeah. Well! We could. I mean… if you wanted to, that is."

The Herb said, "Can if you like."

We took Jack and Polly again. Mum was pleased and said that if I would do it every day she'd up my pocket money. I told her sternly that I would think about it.

While we were walking round the park I asked the Herb whether she reckoned I looked like Brendan Fraser. She said, "Who's Brendan Fraser?"

I said, "The man that played the lead in *The Mummy.*"

"Oh, I *love* that movie!" said the Herb. "I love that bit where all the dead guys come back to life, and the bit where all the beetles get into people's bodies and you see them moving up towards the brain… all the little lumps under the skin, all wriggling and wobbling... blonk, blonk, *aaargh*!" The Herb clutched at her throat. "They've got me!"

Before I could stop myself I said, "I had a dream the other night about beetles."

"What, getting into people's brains?" The Herb staggered, dramatically, and almost tripped over Polly. "Go away, dog! I'm full of beetles!"

"They were after us," I said. "I was rescuing you."

"Rescuing me?" She narrowed her eyes. "Why couldn't I rescue myself?"

I knew I had to think quickly. So I did! It's amazing the speed at which the brain can function when it's under attack. "You'd sprained your ankle," I said. "You couldn't walk."

"I could have hopped."

"Not fast enough."

"I can hop fast!"

Next thing I know, she's walloping off across the grass on one foot, with Jack and Polly bouncing along beside her.

"See?" She walloped back again. "I wouldn't have needed anyone to rescue me!"

I said, "That's what you think. You weren't there! If I hadn't have carried you—"

"*Carried* me? You couldn't carry me!"

"Wanna bet?"

"Yeah, go on! I dare you!"

You can't say no to a dare; even I know that. Even if I am a geek. All I can say is, the Herb may not be very big but she is certainly somewhat heavy. Well, seems to me she's somewhat heavy, or maybe I'm just not very good at carrying people. We ended up in a heap on the grass, with the dogs jumping all over us and the Herb giggling, and me—

I'm not sure I want to write about me. It gave me very weird and peculiar feelings, being in a heap with the Herb.

"Told you you couldn't do it!" said the Herb. "Bet I could carry you easier 'n you could carry me!"

Hah! That is where she was *well* wrong. We ended up in more of a heap than before. The dogs, needless to say, went crazy, but I was kind of glad they were there. Even Russells have their uses.

"Anyway, what d'you reckon?" I said, when we'd got up out of our heap and were back to normal, just me and the Herb, walking round the park. "D'you reckon I look like him or not?"

The Herb said, "Like who? Oh! That *Mummy* man. No, course you don't! Why? Who said you did?"

"One of the Microdot's friends." I gave a little laugh, or tried to. Little laughs aren't that easy, I suspect they probably need a bit of practice. "Linzi," I said. "She's got this thing about me."

"Pathetic," said the Herb. "When d'you want to do some more digging? Tomorrow?"

I said, "Could. But it's OK cos Aaron's coming Monday and so's your friend Lottie. We should be able to get loads done."

I thought that as she and Lottie are such good mates she'd be pleased to hear this, but instead she gave me a look like a dark black cloud and said, "Since when is she coming?"

"Since yesterday," I said. "When we were watching the football. Didn't she tell you?"

"No, she didn't," said the Herb. "You must be mad! How d'you think we're all going to fit in?"

"We could always dig in relays," I said.

The Herb said, "*Relays?*"

I could tell she wasn't happy about it. I don't know what's come over people just lately. First Aaron, now the Herb. Everyone's going all peculiar.

"She doesn't have to come if you don't want," I said.

The Herb sniffed. "*I* don't care! What's it to me? It's your hole. If you don't mind it being trampled all over by a huge horde of people, that's up to you."

"She's really keen," I said. "She really wants to help."

"All *right*. I *said*. I don't *care!*"

I've obviously upset her, but I can't work out how. I can't seem to do anything right, these days. When I got in, Mum had a go at me, saying my bedroom looked like a festering heap. She said she dreaded to think what might be growing there, under all the rubbish. I told her that it wasn't rubbish, and the fact that she had *called* it rubbish just went to show that she didn't know what she was talking about. Wee Scots then started up, telling me I should be ashamed of myself.

"Speaking to your puir mother like that!"

"That's how he speaks to everyone," said the Microdot. "When he *bothers* to speak. He walked right past Linzi today without even saying hallo!"

"I didn't see her," I said.

"You did, you looked straight at her! You are just so *rude* it's unbelievable. You have no manners at all! I wish I'd never introduced you to her."

I said, "That makes two of us."

She immediately started shrieking. "You pig! You loathsome, evil pig!"

"I don't need this," said Mum. "Anna, go and answer that telephone. If it's for the cattery I'll speak to them, if it's anyone else tell them I'm out. Dory, I suggest you spend the evening clearing up your bedroom. If there isn't a clear path from the door to the windows by this time tomorrow, I'm hiring a skip. You know what that means."

She's always threatening to dump my stuff in a skip. She seems incapable of understanding that my room is like a filing system. To her it may look like mess and muddle, but that is just her ignorance. I know *exactly* what is there and where to find it. If I start clearing up, the whole system will collapse!

The Microdot came back from the telephone saying that the call hadn't been for Mum but for her.

139

"It was my boyfriend."

Boyfriend? I didn't know she had one! Mum obviously didn't, either.

"What boyfriend?" she said.

"Rory Sandler. But he isn't any more." The Microdot gave this sad little smile and shook her head. "I've had to ditch him. He has this terrible problem controlling his rage."

I should think anyone would have trouble controlling their rage, going round with her.

seven

Sunday

This time, she said I didn't have to write things down, it was going to be a "verbal test".

"I'm going to ask you three questions, and you've got to give me the answers. You can just *tell* them to me. OK? Cos I don't want you stopping and thinking up something stupid, like you usually do. Question number one." She opened up her little notebook. "What would you do if you won a million pounds?"

I said, "Spend it."

"What on?"

I said, "Is that the second question?"

"No, it's the first one!"

"In that case I've answered it. You said what would I do, and I told you. What's next?"

She glowered at me, but I was in no mood to be messed around by a ten-year old. The worm had turned!

"I'm warning you," I said. "Just get on with it!"

She huffed a bit, and puffed a bit, but obviously thought better of it.

"Question number two... what would you like to be doing in ten years' time?"

I said, "Spending my million pounds."

She breathed, very deeply. I saw her nostrils flare. But she didn't say anything. She didn't dare!

"Question number three... what is your ambition in life?"

I said, "To spend a million pounds. Is that the lot? Can I go now?"

She pursed her lips. "Don't you want to know what it shows?"

I said, "Not really." But of course, she had to tell me.

"Shows you think about nothing but money! I s'ppose that's why you're so horrid to poor Linzi all the

142

time, cos her mum and dad aren't rich... You're just totally *missionary*!"

"For your information," I said, "the word is mercenary, not missionary."

It made me feel quite good, having the last word for once. I begin to think I should have been firmer with her all along.

Monday

Got caught by Sheri Stringer on my way to school this morning. She sort of jumped out at me from a shop doorway; I thought for a minute she was a mugger. She said, "Hi, Dory!" really loud so that a bunch of kids from my class that were walking just a few paces ahead of us all turned to look. Some of them sniggered. I know I'm not imagining it.

When I told Aaron about it later he said they weren't sniggering at me, they were sniggering at Sheri.

"Running after you like that!" He said it's all right for a boy to pursue a girl if he fancies her, but not the other way round. "It's not natural. They just make themselves look silly."

I'm not sure he's right about this; there's a lot of things Aaron's not right about. Seems to me anyone can pursue anyone, doesn't matter whether it's a girl or whether it's a boy. I just wish they wouldn't pursue *me*, cos I find it really embarrassing. I had to walk all the way to school with Sheri giggling and gurgling and waving her eyes about, sort of swivelling them from side to side and making them go all big and shiny, and showing her teeth when she smiled. And *everybody watching.*

Aaron said, "Yeah, it's horrible. Sophy wouldn't ever behave like that."

I said, "Nor would the Herb."

"No. Well! The Herb. If she fancied anyone, she'd probably chuck a brick at 'em. Can't see her ever using fem'nine wiles."

"The Herb's OK," I said. "Don't go having a go at the Herb!"

"I'm not having a go, I'm just saying… she's not like a normal girl."

"Wouldn't want her to be."

"That's all right, then, cos she isn't. You don't have to get on my case!"

"You said it like she was some kind of freak."

"Yeah, well, going round whacking people on the side of the head… I reckon that is a bit freaky."

"Talk about a wimp!" I said. "Didn't have to have stitches, did you? Not as far as I know."

"Another few centimetres it could have got me in the eye. I wouldn't mind," said Aaron, "if it was you did it to me. But it's not what you expect from a girl. Not a normal girl, any rate."

The Herb's been bashing us ever since I can remember. Ever since we all used to play together in the sandpit. I really don't know what's come over Aaron just lately. We never used to quarrel like this. Quarrelling's what the Microdot does, not me and Aaron!

"Anyway," I said, "I hope you're still coming round after school?"

"You have my word," said Aaron. "I am not a person that breaks his word."

We shall see! If he's not here in five minutes, he will be *late.*

Tuesday

Well, he came – and he was on time. That is about as much as I can say. We had a really good dig, but *no thanks at all* to either Aaron or the Herb. They both behaved rather stupidly.

Aaron turned up wearing a saucepan on his head. He told the Herb it was in case she started whacking him again, so then of course she had to pick up a trowel and threaten him with it and next thing I know they're pelting round the garden with five Jack Russells in hot pursuit and all the cats sitting crouched in their chalets watching as they race past. I had to really bawl at them before they took any notice. I don't like to come on heavy, but sometimes they just leave you with no alternative.

"I thought we were here to *dig*?"

"Dig! Yes. Dig!" shouted the Herb. Even then she couldn't resist taking one last whack at the saucepan.

"Now look what you done," said Aaron. "You've gone and put a dent in it!"

If I hadn't got between them they'd have set off all over again. It seems they just get very silly when they're together. Very childish. Aaron kept yelling "Great galloping grandmothers!" for absolutely no reason at all, which I found quite annoying. It's my catch phrase, not his.

He also cried "Great dollops of dog dirt!" Again for no reason. I told him that there couldn't be any dog dirt since the dogs weren't allowed in, but he said it was just an expression.

"Great dollops of dog dirt! Like great galloping grandmothers! Same thing."

"Like this," said the Herb; and she bent herself

double and began galloping in slow-motion on the spot. "See! Look! I'm a galloping granny!"

"And I'm a galloping granddad!"

They giggled and galloped until I told them very sternly to "Either stop it or get out". So they stopped. Only to start up again about two seconds later when Aaron suddenly took it into his head to bellow,

"GREEN GROLLIES!" at the top of his voice. I looked at him, rather hard. He obviously felt my displeasure.

"It's just another expression," he said. "Like, you know! If you were walking down the road for example and saw an elephant coming towards you, you'd go GREEN GROLLIES! you'd go. Sort of, like, to show your amazement. An elephant! Green grollies!"

"On toast," said the Herb. "Here, have some!"

So then they're both pretending to eat, making these disgusting sucking, slurping noises. Yum yum, gurgle guzzle, slippy-slimy *puke*.

They carried on like this the whole time. I don't know why the Herb got so silly; it's not like her. I mean, she can be a bit disrespectful sometimes, making jokes and sending me up, but never this bad. Fortunately her gnome-like friend was there. Lottie. She is a really good worker! Really interested in learning how to dig. I mean, how to dig properly, like a professional. She did everything I told her. No fuss, no smart mouth. Plus she kept checking with me that she was doing it right. Not like Aaron, or even the Herb; they just go at it. Lottie dug really carefully, I was very pleased with her. I made sure, at the end, to let her know. I told her she had worked extremely well, and she gave me this big beam and said that she had enjoyed it. Aaron and the Herb have *never* said they enjoyed it.

Lottie is obviously a very intelligent, sensitive person, in spite of looking like a garden gnome. I said I hoped she would come again, and she said, "Oh, I will! I'd love to!" The Herb, for some reason, scowled. I don't know what her problem is.

Wednesday

At school this morning Aaron said to me, "Y'know that Lottie? I reckon she fancies you."

I told him not to be ridiculous. He said, "I'm not being! She fancies you. 'S obvious. Way she kept looking at you... *oooh, Dory*!" He clasped his hands under his chin and made his voice go all high and flutey. "*Am I doing it right, Dory? Is this how I'm s'pposed to do it, Dory? Tell me, Dory!*"

I said, "She just wanted to help, is all."

Aaron said, "Up a rat's bum!" This is another of his totally meaningless expressions. He told me that I simply wasn't switched on. He said I obviously didn't know the first thing about girls.

"You know about bones and stuff. Fossils and stuff. But when it comes to real everyday sort of stuff you don't know *zilch*."

He has some nerve! If I know zilch, he knows double zilch. *Triple* zilch. I wish he wouldn't talk in this stupid kind of way. I don't want to be fancied! Anyhow, I don't think she does; Lottie, I mean. She is genuinely interested in learning how to conduct a real professional dig. This is what Aaron can't understand. Just because he doesn't have any interest, he finds it impossible to believe that anyone else can.

Thursday

Wasn't able to do any digging at all today. Aaron offered to come round (I think he's feeling guilty after the way he behaved on Tuesday) but I had to say no. Wee Scots is going home tomorrow and wanted to take us all out for dinner. She said it would be nice if just for once we could eat together as a family, instead of in "wee dribs and drabs". Mum said, "Hear, hear!" which I think was a bit hypocritical (if that is the word) considering the number of times she jumps up in the middle of a meal to see to some crisis with a cat. People ring all times of the day and night, expecting her to drop everything and go rushing off, and she always does.

I begged her to let me dig for just an hour and then come to the restaurant by myself – "I can find my way! I know where it is. It's really *urgent* that I get some digging done" – but Mum wouldn't hear of it. She said, "It's your gran's last night and she wants us all to be together. You can do your digging tomorrow."

This is yet another instance of my family not taking me seriously. They seem to think I am digging a hole just for fun. But I'm not! I'm in training for my future. Why can't they see this?

We walked into town through the nature reserve so that Wee Scots could have a look at all the trees and the grass and stuff. She and Mum walked on ahead, with the Microdot bouncing beside them  (showing off, and twirling) leaving me and Dad to amble together in a kind of manly companionship, stern and quiet. Will was somewhere behind. Quite a long way behind, actually, shambling pigeon-toed with his head down, trying to make like he wasn't with us. He's going through what Mum calls "an awkward phase". She says it's something to do with his spots, and him being convinced that no girl will ever look twice at him. Wee Scots says that he must be patient. One of these days he will come into his own.

"He'll be a hunk the same as wee Dory... you see! The lasses will go crazy for him."

I just wish they'd go crazy for him now and leave me alone.

Thinking of girls, whilst strolling manfully by Dad's side, I took the opportunity to ask a question which I had been wanting to ask for some time.

"You know when you and Mum were young?" I said.

"It's going back a bit," said Dad. "But yes, I think I can just about remember it."

"Did Mum ever act all silly?"

Dad said, "Depends what you mean by silly."

"Well, like... giggling, and – and touching, and – coming and *breathing* over you."

"Oh! That sort of silly." Dad chuckled. "Yes, she did that all right."

"What, *Mum*?"

"You'd better believe it!"

"And you didn't mind?"

"I didn't mind," said Dad.

"It didn't upset you?"

"I can't say that it did."

"D'you think Wee Scots ever acted silly?"

"I'd say she probably acted even sillier than your mum!"

"What about Big Nan?"

"Big Nan… no." Dad shook his head. "I can't somehow see her, can you?"

"Had more sense," I said.

"Yes. Well! I suppose that's one way of looking at it."

I was about to ask him what other way there was when a piercing shriek rang out: *"Willy? Where's ma Willy?"*

It was like the whole of the nature reserve just froze. Me and Dad both spun round, thinking that maybe Will had suddenly disappeared, but he was still there, shambling along behind us. A little kid, walking nearby with his mum, tugged at her sleeve and squeaked, "That woman called that man Willy!" His mum immediately went, *"Sh!"* and Will's face turned scarlet. He looked like an over-ripe tomato with purple blotches. I felt really embarrassed for him. I know Wee Scots means well, and I do love her, I love her quite a lot, but I am kind of glad she is going home tomorrow. It was very cruel, what she did to Will. Maybe up in Glasgow it is perfectly normal to screech "Where's wee Willy?" at the top of your voice, but I think she should remember that she is in *England*, now. Things are different here.

I felt quite sorry for Will. I felt that I wanted to comfort him in some way, so I let Dad go on ahead and waited for Will to catch up.

"I've been thinking," I said. "You know all those girls I was going on about?"

I was remembering the conversation I'd had with him, when I complained that they wouldn't leave me alone. Suddenly I could understand why he'd got so mad at me. It must have seemed like I was boasting.

"You know I said how they kept coming and looming over me and everything?"

"Did you?" said Will. "I can't remember."

"Yes, well, I did. Cos they do! And what I was thinking... I was thinking maybe I could sort of, like... pass them on to you. Know what I mean?"

Will said, "No, I don't know what you mean, you patronising little turd! You think I want your cast-offs?"

"Some of them's quite pretty," I said. "Sheri Stringer, f'r instance. Lots of boys fancy Sheri Stringer."

"So think yourself lucky!"

"Yeah, but I'm not interested," I said. "I got other things on my mind. It seems like kind of a waste."

"I'll kind of waste you," said Will, "if you don't belt up!"

All I was doing was just trying to help. He didn't talk to me for the whole of the rest of the evening. He didn't talk to anyone very much. Wee Scots must have really upset him.

Friday

Wee Scots went home this morning and I find that now she has gone I quite miss her. Whenever we got home from school she always used to ask us what we'd been up to.

"And what have ye learned today, laddie?" Or lassie, if it were the Microdot. And then she'd want to test us on stuff that she'd learned when she was at school, like dates for instance. She was really obsessed by dates!

"All right, laddie! The battle of Bannockburrrrn... when was it? Quickly, now! Ye shouldna have tae think."

I quite enjoy a few dates myself, in fact I am rather

good at them, but I have never even heard of the battle of Bannockburn. Wee Scots used to do her nut.

"Och, awa wi' ye! What do they teach you at this school of yours?"

It got so that me and the Microdot, if we arrived home together, started taking it in turns which of us went in at the front and which of us sneaked round the back.

Today when I got in the house was empty. Dad was out delivering some garden furniture, and there was a note from Mum stuck to the fridge saying "Gone to pick up cat. Back soon". I went outside and looked at the mothball necklaces that Wee Scots had made to stop the Russells using the trees as lavatories. I felt really fond of her! She may be the granny from hell, but she is lots more fun than Big Nan.

Dug for an hour; just me and the Herb. The Herb unearthed an unusual bit of rock with a hole going through it. It's not what you'd call important, but it is quite interesting. The Herb got excited and cried, "Is it a trib'lite?" I said, "No, it's just a bit of rock."

"Well, thank *you*," said the Herb. "All my hard work!"

I didn't mean to be ungrateful; I just didn't seem to be in a hole-digging mood. I'd have liked to suggest we went up the park again, but ever since I had my dream I've been feeling self-conscious. Like suppose I suddenly lost control and made a grab at her? At her hand, I mean. She'd go ballistic! She'd bash me, for sure. Not that I'm scared of being bashed, I'm not a wimp like Aaron; I just don't like the thought of the Herb getting mad at me. Somehow the hole seems safer than the park. When I'm digging, I'm *focused*. It's only walking round the park I have these odd feelings.

Anyway, we weren't supposed to be alone; Aaron and Lottie were supposed to be helping. Aaron did actually turn up, but he said he couldn't stop, he had things to do. He didn't say what things.

"Guess he's walking the imaginary dog," I said.

"He's gone soft," said the Herb. "Soft and soppy!"

I said that he had been all right up until just a few weeks ago. "Then all of a sudden he seemed to go peculiar."

"That's the way it happens," said the Herb. "Just suddenly. It's like getting the flu… one minute you're normal, the next you're struck down."

People get over the flu; maybe Aaron will get over Sophy Timms. I am not very hopeful, however. When I suggested it to the Herb she said that now he'd been stricken he'd probably stay that way.

"Even if he gets over her, there'll be others. There isn't any cure."

I wish she hadn't told me that! Aaron is my best mate. The thought of him being permanently stricken is quite upsetting.

To change the subject, I asked the Herb what had happened to Lottie. She said, "Nothing's happened to her. Why do you want to know?"

There was a definite note of aggression in her voice. Nervously –cos you can never be sure, with girls, what you might have said to upset them, even the Herb – I explained that I was just asking.

"She seemed like she was genuinely interested."

The Herb said, "In what? Digging?" and gave this sarcastic bray of laughter.

I said, "Well – yeah. Like she really wanted to learn. I thought she was going to come with you?"

"I told her not to bother."

"Oh." I said *oh* because it was the only thing which immediately occurred to me. The Herb didn't say anything; just went on shovelling earth with her trowel.

"Could have done with an extra pair of hands," I said. "I mean, like, if we're going to get anywhere before Dad wants his bit of garden back."

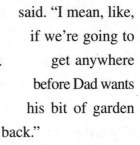

She still didn't say anything. Just pursed her lips and went on shovelling.

"I mean, if Aaron's not going to be coming any more... why did you tell her not to bother, anyway?"

"If you really want to know – " the Herb was going at it like crazy, shovelling for all she was worth "– if you really *have* to know, it's cos she's starting to get silly about you and I know you don't like that sort of thing. So there! Now I've told you. Now you can stop wittering."

I found that really hurtful. I don't *witter*. "All I care about," I said, "is getting the work done."

"Yes, and all she cares about," said the Herb, "is making eyes at you."

"But she's your friend!"

"That's why I told her to stay away." The Herb was bent over her trowel, her face bright red with the effort she was putting in. "You can do that sort of thing with friends. They understand."

I said, "I don't!"

"No, well, you're a boy," said the Herb.

That is the first time she has ever said anything like that to me. You're a *boy*. It hasn't ever mattered before! I've just been me. The Herb's just been the Herb. I don't know what to make of all this.

I have come upstairs with my piece of rock. I am going to examine it most carefully. When I have examined it I shall make some notes and put it with the rest of the artefacts.

There is something very *soothing* about a piece of rock.

eight

Saturday

Questions

No.1 What is the thing you would most like to acheeve by the end of the year?

The latest of her cruddy little tests. She assured me that it was going to be the last one, so I said that it had better be, as I was getting quite sick of them.

She said, "It *is*. I *told* you."

I said, "Yeah, well, it had better be." I then pointed out that in fact the first question was a total nonsense since there isn't any such word as acheeve. I suggested

161

that maybe she meant *achieve*, spelt with an i and an e.

She shrieked, "That's anelephant!"

I said, "It could be a kangaroo, it's still spelt wrong."

She was silent for about two seconds (which is practically a record), then in irritable tones she said, "What are you going on about kangaroos for?"

I said, "Well, you were going on about elephants."

"*An*elephant. It doesn't matter how it's spelt, it's completely anelephant!"

That was when it struck me: she meant *irrelevant*. It cracked me up so much I was bent almost double and couldn't speak for laughing.

Angrily, she said, "*You're* anelephant! You're a total waste of space!"

I felt a bit mean, then, cos she'd gone all red and puckered. She hates it if she thinks someone's making fun of her.

I said, "Oh, give me the stupid thing!" and snatched it from her. "You don't have to watch," I said. "I'll show you when I've finished."

"Well, but you've got to take it seriously."

I said that I would, as I still felt guilty for laughing at her. I guess irrelevant is quite a big word if you're only ten years old.

This is how I answered:

Question: *What is the thing you would most like to acheeve by the end of the year?*

Answer: *Find a dinosaur egg.*

Question: *Who is the person you would most like to acheeve it with?*

Answer: *The Herb.*

Question: *What is the thing you would most like to happen to you?*

Answer: *Go back in time and see a real live dinosaur.*

Question: *If you had one wish for humanity, what would it be?*

Answer: *That girls would stop giggling.*

Question: *Would you rather eat dog dirt or go out with Linzi?*

"Answer it," she said, "answer it!"

"You didn't get that one out of a magazine," I said.

"No, I didn't," she said. "I made that one up specially, and if you don't answer it I'll know you've got something to hide!"

To humour her – as it's the last time – I wrote, *Go out with Linzi.* I thought she'd be pleased. I reckoned it deserved at least a gold star.

"So is that the right answer?" I said.

Gloatingly, she said that it was, but that it was "too late".

"What d'you mean, 'too late'?"

"She doesn't want to go out with you any more. She wouldn't go out with you if you fell on your bended knees and *begged* her! She's gone off of you. She's got a crush on someone else."

"That's a relief," I said.

"Don't you want to know who it is?"

"Don't care, so long as it's not me."

"It's your friend Joey."

I said, "Joe Icard?"

"He's your friend, isn't he?"

Yes, he is, and he's never mentioned anything to me about some silly little Year 6 having a crush on him.

"I'm not making it up," said the Microdot. "She thinks he's really cute. She used to think you were, but she's decided there's more to people than just the way they look."

"Does he know about it?" I said.

"Course he knows about it!" scoffed the Microdot. "He's not blind – not like some people. He *smiles* at her. He doesn't walk past and ignore her. He likes girls. You're only interested in your nerdy dinosaurs. What's this about *girls stopping giggling*?"

I said, "That's my wish for humanity."

164

"You mean, you just want everyone to be *miserable*?"

"I wouldn't be miserable," I said.

"Everyone else would! That is such a *sick* answer."

"So what did you put? What's your great wish for humanity?"

She drew herself up to her full height (about ten centimetres).

"World peace," she said.

Oh, spare me!

"I'm going to go away, now, and do your profile. I can tell you already," she said, "it's not looking good!"

I dunno why she's got it in for me. I once heard Mum explaining to Wee Scots that we were too close in age and it made us competitive. But I'm not competitive! It's the Microdot that always has to be one up. I just want to be left alone to get on with my life. What's so wrong with that?

I know she's going to tell me I'm weird and geeky, all because I'd rather dig for dinosaur remains than go out with girls. It's not that I have anything against girls! I know that they are necessary, and I even quite like some of them. Lottie, for instance. We got on OK! And, of course, the Herb. We've always got on.

Come to think of it, the Herb's a bit of a giggler; she giggles quite a lot. I wouldn't want her to stop doing it! But the Herb's different. She's not like other girls, she's – well! She's the Herb.

Dad reminded me this evening that this weekend is my last weekend for the hole. "Come Monday, it all gets filled in!"

"And don't forget," said Mum, "next Saturday and Sunday are *out*. OK?"

I said, "Yes. OK," trying not to heave a sigh.

Saturday is Gran and Granddad's golden wedding anniversary. They will have been married for fifty years! There is going to be a big party, with lots of people coming from all over. I am quite looking forward to it, though I can't help thinking of all the digging I could get done if I didn't have to go. Unfortunately Mum insists.

"Of course you have to go! Miss your gran and granddad's golden wedding? No way!"

I suppose I wouldn't want to, really; it will probably be quite fun. It is being held in a hall which Dad and Uncle Clive have hired. It is going to go on practically all day. It seems strange to have a party in the daytime, but Gran and Granddad are too old, I guess, to stay awake in the evening.

They are spending the night with Uncle Clive and Auntie Jess, where there are no Jack Russells to upset them, then on Sunday we are all going out for a family lunch, before driving Gran and Granddad back to Eastbourne. By the time we get home it will be too late to do any digging. I am really going to miss my hole!

Monday

This morning, at school, I had a long talk with Joe on the subject of girls. I started off by asking him about Linzi. I said, "Did you know my sister's friend has a crush on you?"

He denied all knowledge! He said, "Who is she? Who told you?"

Bitterly, I said, "My sister." I should have known better than to pay any attention to the Microdot. "Just forget about it," I said. "She's nuts!"

But he didn't seem to want to forget about it. He said, "So who is she, then?" I told him she was in Year 6 and that according to the Microdot – not that she can be trusted – he had actually smiled at her.

"Oh! Yeah. I remember. She's the one with the plaits."

"She has got plaits," I said. "Yes."

"Hangs around in a bunch by the gate."

"Yes."

A big grin suddenly split his face. "I did sort of smile at her. Cos she smiled at me, you know? Wouldn't have been polite not to smile back. Anyone would've. Even you would've."

I couldn't think what to say to this. What did he mean, even I would have?

"It's only natural. It's only *normal*." He looked at me, earnestly. "You can't just ignore them."

"What," I said, "girls?"

"That's right! You gotta get along."

I said, "I do get along."

"Yeah, but more than just like… *getting along*. You gotta—"

"What?"

"Well! Like – mingle, an' – an' talk an' – show 'em you care. That kind of stuff."

I'd never have thought of Joe as being someone that would want to mingle and talk. He's always been what

Mum calls "a bit of a lad". The grin broke out again, right across his face.

"You're saying she's got this crush on me?"

I told him that that was what the Microdot was saying. "Only I dunno how reliable she is. Sometimes she makes things up."

"No, I reckon she's gotta be right. Way she looked at me… what d'you say her name was? Lindy?"

"Linzi."

"Linzi…" He rolled it lovingly off his tongue. "Linzi what?"

"I dunno."

"Ask your sister. Ask her what her name is and where she lives."

"Why? What d'you want to know for?"

"If someone's got a crush on me," said Joe, "I need to know about 'em, don't I?"

I shook my head. I couldn't make any sense of this conversation.

"You'd just better watch it," I said. "You give her any encouragement, she'll start making a right nuisance of herself."

He waved a hand. "I can cope."

"But she giggles," I said.

"I like 'em when they giggle! Think she'd go out with me?"

"She's Year *6*," I said.

"Year 6 is good. You might think Year 8, but forget about it. They're rubbish! Reckon they know everything. Even Year 7 can get a bit above themselves. Cal went out with Janine Edwards last week. Know what she said to him? Said he was too young for her. Didn't have enough experience. She's got some nerve!"

I said, "*Janine Edwards*?" She was the great lumping girl that fell on me in the PE cupboard.

Joe said, "You'd better believe it! Take it from me, Year 6 are the ones to go for. They are *the best*!"

I found the whole discussion somewhat alarming. Not only Joe, taking an interest in the Microdot's little giggly friend, but Calum, going out with Janine Edwards and *nobody telling me*. When I asked Joe why nobody had told me, he said, "Didn't think you'd want to know. Anyway, he's not going with her again. Says he doesn't want to be insulted. Maybe your sister would like to go out with him? She's not bad looking."

I said, "No, but she's very bad-tempered."

I don't want the Microdot going out with one of my mates. No way! And why would they *want* to go out with her? All of a sudden, life is very confusing. Once upon a time it used to seem so simple. There was me and Aaron, and Joe and Calum, and, of course, the Herb. Now there's only me and the Herb, and even she has started acting strange just lately, not letting Lottie come and dig, telling me I was a *boy*. What did she mean by that? Why did she say it? I can't understand! I can't understand anything any more. I am beginning to feel quite depressed.

Thursday

Did a bit of digging after school today. Just me and the Herb. It is probably the last real digging we shall be able to do. The Herb said, "It's a pity Aaron isn't here."

I said, "Pity Lottie isn't here."

I said it without thinking. The Herb instantly banged down her trowel and gave me this long, hard look. "Do you *want* her to be here?"

I said, "No!" I could almost hear the terror in my voice. The Herb can be quite scary.

171

"So why did you say it was a pity?"

"I just meant…you know! We'd get a big more digging done. That's all."

"If you *want* her here," said the Herb, "I'll *ring* her. You only have to *say*. If you really can't *live* without having her – if you're likely to go into some kind of *decline*—"

"I'm not!"

"Just *tell* me. All right? Cos I don't want to be responsible for you having this massive mental breakdown all because *Lottie* isn't here. I can get her here! No problem. You want me to get her here?"

"No!"

"Then why keep on about her?"

I protested that I wasn't. I wasn't keeping on! "It's just… you said about Aaron, so I said about Lottie." She obviously doesn't want her coming; I don't know why. Maybe they have stopped being friends. Girls do seem to quarrel a lot more than boys, at least if the Microdot is anything to go by. Except that the Microdot is a very quarrelsome sort of person, which I didn't think the Herb was. It is very confusing.

"Let's just *dig*," said the Herb. "And stop keeping *on*!"

We dug for just over an hour. The Herb worked really well, she is definitely better without Aaron. For

172

the first time in ages, we uncovered an artefact. It is an old soap dish, made of some kind of metal. It has a top half and a bottom half and is greyish in colour. At first glance, it looks a bit like a hand grenade. The Herb actually thought it was a hand grenade. She shouted, "Take cover!" and hurled herself to the ground with her hands over her head, so that all the Russells got madly excited and started barking, and jumping up and down.

I am glad to say that I *did not panic.* I picked up the soap dish and hurled it as hard as I could out of the cage and into the bushes before flinging myself down, *on top of the Herb,* and waiting for the bang. I am quite pleased with the way I behaved as I have often wondered what I would do in an emergency.

It *could* have been a hand grenade; it's the sort of thing you read about. **LOCAL MAN FINDS UNEXPLODED BOMB IN BACK GARDEN**.

The Herb was quite disappointed. She said, "A hand grenade would at least have been exciting. We haven't discovered *anything* exciting! Not even a trib'lite."

I said, "Trilobite."

"Whatever! You still haven't got one. All you've got is a mouldy old soap dish!"

It's true, I would have liked to find a trilobite; I suppose I have been secretly hoping. I've even wondered if Dad might be persuaded to let me get rid of the compost heap and dig under that. But just at this moment I'm not really too concerned; I have other things on my mind. Worrying things. When I flung myself at the Herb, to protect her from the hand grenade, I had this weird urge to kiss her. *Kiss the Herb.* I am going red just thinking about it. I don't know what's happening to me! What is going on here?

I used to be so happy, just digging my hole and thinking about dinosaurs. Now I'm all hot and bothered and embarrassed.

The Herb won't be able to come over tomorrow as she has to stay home and help Auntie Jess prepare for Gran and Granddad. She is *not best pleased*, as Gran would say.

"Every time they visit it's like we're expecting the Queen, or something." She said bitterly that it was all right for me. "You've got a secret weapon."

She meant the Russells. I said, "Maybe you should get some."

"I suggested that," said the Herb. "Mum says we can't, cos of her being out at work all day."

"There's cats," I said; but cats aren't as intrusive as dogs. They don't bounce, and they don't bark. Big Nan could probably cope with cats. "At least," I said, "the party should be fun."

"*Huh!*" said the Herb.

I feel for her, I really do; I know what it's like, having Big Nan to stay. But I am kind of relieved that we won't be down in the hole again. Not if I'm going to have these wild urges.

It's very unsettling.

nine

Saturday

Today was Gran and Granddad's golden wedding celebration. Mum got us all up really early – and we then arrived *late*. This was thanks to the Microdot having a crisis with clothes. She came trailing downstairs in her dressing gown, clutching some kind of pink garment and going, "Mum, it's got a mark!" A great big splodge, all down the front. I suggested she should wear it the other way round, so the mark was at the back, but she turned on me and screamed that I was an idiot.

"People would think I'd sat in dog poo!"

I said, "So wear something else," but according to her she hasn't got anything.

"Everything else is rubbish!"

"Ever thought about a bin bag?" I said.

"Dory, stop it," said Mum. "Anna, let me have a look."

Mum and Dad are such a soft touch where the Microdot is concerned. I don't know whether it's because she's small, or whether it's because she's the youngest, or whether it's simply because she's a girl, but they let her get away with stuff that me and Will would never be allowed to get away with. Like I can just imagine, if I started wailing that I had to go and do some last-minute digging in the hole, the reaction would be totally *negative*. It'd be, "Dory, don't you dare, "Dory, get a move on," "Dory, we're going." But was it "Anna, stop being so vain" or "Anna, we haven't got time"? No. It wasn't. It was, "Oh, darling, what a horrible mark! Wherever did that come from? Let's quickly pop it in the machine."

So we all sat around and waited for half an hour, and even then they wouldn't let me go and dig. Will, for some reason, seemed to think it was funny. He said, "She's got more clothes than the rest of us put together!"

"I know," said Mum. "But it's a big day, and she's set her heart on wearing this dress."

I could have said that I'd set my heart on doing some last-minute digging, but I didn't bother. They've never taken my digging seriously; to them it's just always been a joke.

"We are *going* to be *late*," I said.

"Not by much," said Dad. "Be patient! It's important for little girls to look their best."

Well! If that isn't a sexist remark, I'd like to know what is. The Microdot, who prides herself on being some kind of hot shot feminist, just sat there, smirking. I felt so glad that the Herb isn't like that, making a fuss about clothes, and hair, and all the little bits and pieces the Microdot likes to have stuck on her, or hanging off her, or just generally attached to her. I thought the Herb would probably turn up wearing a T-shirt and jeans, same as usual. Or even her boiler suit. Good old Herb!

"There," said Dad, when at last the Microdot was all kitted out and ready to go. "I'd say that was worth the wait!"

"Still look better in a bin bag," I said.

"Yes, and you'd look better locked in the cellar with the lights out!" shrieked the Microdot. "And *for* your information," she added, "I'm working on your profile and it's coming out *seriously weird*. Cos that's what you are!"

"Oh, people, please," said Mum. "Not today! Let's just try to have a good time, shall we?"

When we got to the hall, the car park was crammed with cars; I couldn't believe how many. And then we went inside and could hardly move for bodies. Uncle Clive said later that over fifty people had come! Some of them were old friends of Gran and Granddad – *really* old, in some cases. Practically ancient – and some were family, like great-grandnieces and third cousins twice removed, come all the way over from Canada and Australia. We had to go round being introduced, with the Microdot acting all girly in her pink dress, and Dad saying things like, "Good grief! Last time we met you were still at the crawling stage." Just once or twice, people even said it to Dad.

I kept searching for the Herb, but couldn't see her anywhere. And then we bumped into Auntie Jess (looking stressed) and I said, "Where's the Herb?" and she pointed and said, "Over there… sulking." I still couldn't see her. There was a girl in some sort of blue get-up, munching on a sausage roll, but no Herb. And then it struck me… that *was* the Herb. The girl in the blue get-up. That was the Herb!

I immediately pushed my way over there. I said, "Hi!"

The Herb mumbled back "Hi" through a mouthful of sausage roll.

"I've been looking all over for you!"

"Can't have looked very hard."

"It's just... I didn't recognise you," I said. "Dressed like that."

The Herb scowled. She said, "You don't have to *stare*. It's really rude to stare."

I said, "I'm not staring."

"Excuse me, your eyes are practically on stalks."

I felt my cheeks go flaming into the red zone. I don't very often blush, but the Herb in a dress was making me feel kind of bashful. I'm not sure quite why. Maybe because I'm not used to seeing her all done up like that. Even her hair looked different, like it had been styled, or something. She didn't look like the Herb. She looked really pretty!

"You took your time getting here," she said.

I said, "Yeah, it was that Microdot... she found a mark on her dress and had to have it washed. Said it was the only thing she could possibly wear. Personally I reckon she'd do better in a bin bag."

The Herb looked across to where the Microdot was peacocking around, doing little twirls and showing off.

"It's *pink*," she said.

I said, "Tell me about it!"

"At least mine's not *pink*."

"No, yours is OK," I said. "Yours is blue." And then, absolutely without meaning to, I added, "Matches your eyes." And then I blushed, furiously, and so did the Herb.

"It was my mum," she said. "She made me wear it. Stupid thing!"

I said, "What, your mum?"

"No! The stupid dress."

"It's nice," I said. And then, of course, I blushed even more, cos I've never in my life said anything soppy like that to the Herb.

She snarled, "It's not nice, it's *stupid*. I hate wearing dresses!"

That was when Mum came over. "Hallo, Rosie!" she said. "You're looking very attractive!"

Mum shouldn't have said that. Poor old Herb! She scowled so hard her face went all scrunched and puckered like one of next door's garden gnomes. Even then, Mum didn't know when to stop.

"Lovely to see you in a dress, for a change! You should do it more often," she said.

Mum can be *really* tactless at times.

The party went on all day. The best bit was the food. Long tables all covered in it, down one whole side of the hall. You could just stand and eat non-stop, if you had the room. Me and the Herb kept meeting up by the sausage rolls and the little bits of things on sticks. Normally we'd have stuck together, cos me and the Herb, we're never short of stuff to talk about. Not normally, we're not. Today, I dunno why, we both got tongue-tied. It was the dress that did it: the Herb didn't seem like the Herb any more. She seemed more like – well. Like a *girl.* And I don't know how to talk to girls!

It made me think glumly that maybe the Microdot was right: maybe I am seriously weird. Nobody else seems to have these problems. Not even Aaron. Not even Joe and Calum. Not even Will, in spite of his spots. Ever since we arrived he'd been busy chatting up this girl that was the granddaughter of a great, great something or other. Aunt, uncle, cousin; whatever. She and Will were really hitting it off. She kept beaming at him, and making her eyes go all big. I felt pleased for Will, cos I knew how anxious he'd been, but I couldn't help wondering what he was saying to her. What did he find to talk about? I wouldn't know where to begin!

I grabbed a handful of sausage rolls and stood eating them behind a nearby pillar, trying to listen in – not to eavesdrop, just to *learn* – but Will caught sight of me and got a bit vicious. He told me to "Go and stuff yourself somewhere else, can't you? Spitting crumbs all over the place!" So I went back to the other side of the room where I found the Herb mooching about by herself, still scowling. I said, "Look at Will and that girl. What d'you think they're talking about?"

"No idea," said the Herb.

She definitely wasn't in a communicative mood.

At six o'clock the party broke up. A few of us – Gran and Granddad, Uncle Clive and Auntie Jess, me and the Herb, Mum and Dad and the Microdot, plus a couple of ancients – went back to the Herb's house. *Will did not come with us.*

"Where's he gone?" I said.

"*He's* got a girlfriend," said the Microdot. "Her name's Barney. She's really nice."

I said, "But he only met her this morning!"

"So what?" said the Microdot.

I hadn't realised it could happen that quickly. Will must be a really fast worker!

"I did his profile last night," said the Microdot. "He scores practically top marks for being sociable. I'm still working on yours."

"I know," I said. "You told me."

"I'll probably finish it some time tomorrow. It doesn't look – *where are you going?*"

"Going to find the Herb," I said.

"But I'm talking to you!"

"Too bad. Talk to me some other time."

The Herb was in the kitchen with Auntie Jess. They had obviously been having some kind of a disagreement cos I heard Auntie Jess say, "…doesn't hurt you just for *once,*" in quite cross tones. And then I came in and she snatched up a tray full of plates and glasses and went swishing out into the hall.

The Herb was standing by the sink. Scowling.

"Something wrong?" I said.

"What is *wrong*," said the Herb, "is that a person can't wear what a person wants to wear… it's like living in a *police* state! All I said was could I get out of this puke-making dress now, and she goes raving berserk. *I bought that dress specially, surely for once you could make me proud of you…* I've been stuck in the stupid thing all day! I'm *sick* of it."

It didn't seem quite the moment for telling her it looked pretty. I had this feeling she wouldn't react too well. I didn't want to get whacked.

"Will's gone off with that girl," I said. "Her name's Barney, she—"

"Let's you and me go off!" The Herb grabbed the back door handle and wrenched the door open. "Let's go round your place and dig!"

"What," I said, "now?"

"Yes, now! You want to find a trib'lite, don't you? Well, come on, then!"

She grabbed my arm and pulled me after her, into the garden. We scooted round the side and out through the front gate, up the road and round the corner. We didn't stop till we reached Warrington Crescent. The back gate was locked, so we had to climb over.

"Just do it *quietly*," I whispered, "or you'll get the

dogs barking."

Giggling, the Herb hoisted herself up. I opened my mouth to say, "Watch your dress," but I wasn't quite brave enough. I did feel a bit alarmed when she galloped ahead of me up the garden and jumped straight down into the hole, but then I jumped into the hole with her and we got digging, and I forgot she was all dressed up. She was just good old Herb, same as usual.

We dug and we dug, more than we've ever dug before. We uncovered a bit of old iron, and an interesting piece of flint, but nothing of real significance (as we professionals say).

"No trib'lites," said the Herb.

"Doesn't matter," I said. "It was still fun."

We stood there, knee deep, in the hole.

"You thought it was fun," I said, "didn't you?" I was suddenly anxious to know. I would have hated to think she had only been humouring me all this time. "What I mean is… do you really actually *enjoy* it?"

She said, "Course I do! Better 'n being stuck indoors, any rate."

It made me happy when she said that. Eagerly I told her that I was going to ask Dad if I could get rid of the compost heap. "Then we can start another one!"

"Another compost heap?"

"Another hole."

"Oh! Right."

"If I do," I said, "d'you want to come and dig it with me?"

"Yeah, I'll come and dig it with you," said the Herb.

"I won't ask Lottie! Not if you'd rather I didn't. And maybe I won't bother asking Aaron, either. Maybe it'll just be our hole, that we dig together."

The Herb said, "Our very own hole."

"Yeah! What d'you reckon?"

"I reckon that would be really neat," said the Herb. "A hole of our own." And then, for absolutely no reason that I could see, she gave this great shriek of laughter.

I said, "What? What's funny?"

"You are!" said the Herb.

The Herb has always had this strange sense of humour. She laughs at the oddest things. Rather sternly I asked her if she knew that she had got mud all over her dress. "Great gobbets of it."

"So what?" she said. "It's only a stupid dress."

"But it's all over," I said. "And I think you've gone and torn it, as well."

"Torn it?" That got to her. "Where? Where?"

"At the back," I said.

She spun round, trying to see it. "Omigod!" Her voice came out in a strangulated squawk. "Mum'll go ballistic!"

It's the first time I have ever, *ever* known the Herb come close to panic. She is just not a panicky sort of person. But I know what it's like when mums go ballistic. It's like, everyone scatter! Mum on the warpath!

"She'll kill me," wailed the Herb. "She'll say I did it on purpose!"

"Don't worry," I said. "I'll tell her it was my fault."

"She'll never believe you!"

"She will, I'll make her. I'll say it was all my idea, we had to come and dig before Dad took his bit of garden back. They'll go for that. They all think I'm mad and geeky. Everybody does."

"I don't," said the Herb. "I sometimes think you're a bit *mad*, but I've never thought you were geeky. If you were geeky you wouldn't be offering to sacrifice yourself."

Sacrifice. That was a good word.

"Deeje, you can't," said the Herb. "I won't let you!"

"Got no choice," I said. "Gonna do it whether you let me or not."

189

In my dream I'd rescued her from rampaging beetles. Now I was rescuing her from the wrath of Auntie Jess – which I reckon was just as heroic, in its own way, cos Mum had a right go at me later. "How could you?" and "Totally inconsiderate!" and "So ashamed of you," etc. She was pretty damn mad.

Carelessly I told the Herb it was no big deal. "Just leave it to me. I'll sort things out."

"You're serious," said the Herb. "You really mean it!" Suddenly, without any warning, she lunged forward and squashed my face between her hands. Before I knew what she was doing, she had planted a big kiss on my lips – well, partly on my lips. I think I must have moved at the wrong moment, cos part of it went on my nose. "Oh, Deeje, that is so sweet of you!" she said.

No one has ever told me that I'm sweet before; it kind of knocked me out. Specially coming from the Herb, cos she's not into soppy talk. I think it knocked her out a bit, too. We stood there together in the hole, like wondering what had hit us. In the end I said rather gruffly that maybe we ought to be getting back now. I don't know why I said it gruffly; it's just the way it came out.

"I mean, we *could* stay on a bit," I said, "'cept I don't

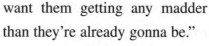

want them getting any madder than they're already gonna be."

The Herb said, "No. Absolutely not!"

As we were walking back up the Crescent, she took my hand. *The Herb.* Holding my hand! I always thought she'd be angrier than a hornet if I tried doing that.

"I'm really sorry we didn't find any trib'lites," she said.

I told her that it really didn't matter. And it really didn't; not at that moment.

I'm thinking now that I still would like to find some. But maybe Dad will let me dig under the compost heap – and the Herb will be there to help me. cos she enjoys it! She said she did.

We won't dig all of the time, of course. I mean, there are other things in life, such as going up the park, for instance. I reckon we'll probably be going up the park quite a lot. If the Herb wants to, that is.

But I think she will! That is definitely the feeling I have.

I'm glad I didn't let Auntie Jess get mad at her, even if it did mean suffering the cruel lash of Mum's tongue. It's made me feel a lot less geeky.